WITHDRAWN

My Life as a Ninja

Other Books by Janet Tashjian, Illustrated by Jake Tashjian

The Einstein the Class Hamster Series:
Einstein the Class Hamster
Einstein the Class Hamster and the Very Real Game Show
Einstein the Class Hamster Saves the Library

The My Life Series:
My Life as a Book
My Life as a Stuntboy
My Life as a Cartoonist
My Life as a Joke
My Life as a Gamer
My Life as a Ninja
My Life as a Youtuber
My Life as a Meme

by Janet Tashjian

Fault Line
For What It's Worth
Marty Frye, Private Eye
Multiple Choice
Tru Confessions

The Larry Series:
The Gospel According to Larry
Vote for Larry
Larry and the Meaning of Life

The Sticker Girl Series:
Sticker Girl
Sticker Girl Rules the School
Sticker Girl and the Cupcake Challenge

Praise for **My Life as a Book:**

★ "Janet Tashjian, known for her young adult novels, offers a novel that's part Diary of a Wimpy Kid, part intriguing mystery.... Give this to kids who think they don't like reading. It might change their minds."

—*Booklist*, starred review

★ "Dryly hilarious first-person voice.... A kinder, gentler Wimpy Kid with all the fun and more plot."

—*Kirkus Reviews*, starred review

Praise for **My Life as a Stuntboy:**

"A fast-moving plot and relatable protagonist make this stand-alone sequel a good choice for boys."

—*School Library Journal*

"Fans of the first will be utterly delighted by this sequel and anxious to see what Derek will turn up as next."

—*The Bulletin*

Praise for **My Life as a Cartoonist:**

"Great for reluctant readers (like Derek), this also neatly twists the bullying theme, offering discussion possibilities." —*Booklist*

"This entertaining read leaves some provoking questions unanswered—usefully."

—*Kirkus Reviews*

Praise for **My Life as a Joke:**

"At times laugh-out-loud funny.... Its solid lesson, wrapped in high jinks, gives kids something to think about while they giggle."

—*Booklist*

JANET TASHJIAN

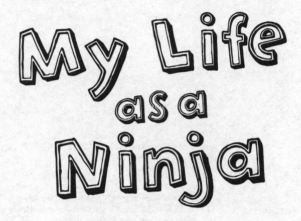

with cartoons by
JAKE TASHJIAN

SQUARE
FISH
Christy Ottaviano Books
Henry Holt and Company
New York

SQUARE
FISH

An imprint of Macmillan Publishing Group, LLC
175 Fifth Avenue, New York, NY 10010
mackids.com

MY LIFE AS A NINJA. Text copyright © 2017 by Janet
Tashjian. Illustrations copyright © 2017 by Jake Tashjian.
All rights reserved. Printed in the United States of America by
LSC Communications, Harrisonburg, Virginia.

Square Fish and the Square Fish logo are trademarks of
Macmillan and are used by Henry Holt and Company under
license from Macmillan.

Our books may be purchased in bulk for promotional,
educational, or business use. Please contact your local
bookseller or the Macmillan Corporate and Premium Sales
Department at (800) 221-7945 ext. 5442 or by email at
MacmillanSpecialMarkets@macmillan.com.

Library of Congress Cataloging-in-Publication Data is available.
ISBN 978-1-250-29415-9 (paperback)
ISBN 978-1-62779-890-7 (ebook)

Originally published in the United States by Henry Holt
and Company
First Square Fish edition, 2019
Book designed by Patrick Collins
Square Fish logo designed by Filomena Tuosto

10 9 8 7 6 5 4 3 2 1

AR: 5.3 / LEXILE: 850L

For Cinder—

Best. Dog. Ever.

My Life as a Ninja

War Cry

"Cowabunga!" I jump out from behind the credenza, blocking my mother's path as she walks by with a stack of mail.

credenza

"Derek! You have to stop scaring me!" She sprints across the room to pick up the envelopes falling to the floor.

sprints

Ever since my friends and I were lucky enough to test the Arctic Ninja video game for Global Games, we've

climate

bewildered

been obsessed with ninjas. The game took place in the Arctic but my friends and I live in Los Angeles, so the climate is a lot different.

Mom tries to reach a stray paper that fell underneath the couch. "I'm pretty sure *cowabunga* is a surfer word and not a ninja war cry."

My bewildered mother doesn't realize it's also Michelangelo's catchphrase from *Teenage Mutant Ninja Turtles*. Lately my friends and I have been moving away from turtle culture to REAL ninjas. And that means reading a lot of graphic novels from Japan.

With my reading disability, longer books can sometimes be difficult so I like novels with lots of illustrations. I've been drawing my vocabulary words since elementary school and always look for a way to connect words to pictures.

When Mom suggests watching a martial arts movie after dinner, I jump at the chance. Literally.

My dive from the pantry to the couch spills my mom's paperwork all over again.

"Derek, stop!"

But stopping is the last thing I'll do.

In fact, I'm just getting started.

My Ninja Friends

consumed

research

Because Matt, Umberto, Carly, and I are equally consumed with the world of ninjas, we check out martial arts classes to take together. Carly did the research, of course, looking for the closest school with the best program.

"There's one in Santa Monica with a famous sensei." She turns to me. "*Sensei* means 'teacher.'"

"I KNOW WHAT SENSEI MEANS!

Just because I'm not a good reader doesn't mean I'm stupid."

Carly rolls her eyes. "I'm not saying you're stupid. I just didn't think you knew Japanese."

Matt comes to my defense. "Derek eats sushi, doesn't he? Of course he knows Japanese."

The day hasn't even started and already Carly's had it with Matt and me. Umberto pulls up in his wheelchair just in time to change the subject.

"Did you hear Ms. McCoddle's looking for a volunteer to run the class play?"

Carly's ears perk up. If there's ever a chance to impress a teacher or get extra credit, Carly is first in line. She asks Umberto for details.

revolution

colonists

miniature

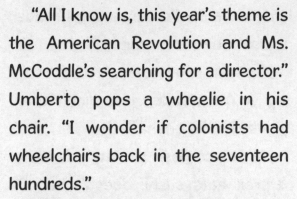

"All I know is, this year's theme is the American Revolution and Ms. McCoddle's searching for a director." Umberto pops a wheelie in his chair. "I wonder if colonists had wheelchairs back in the seventeen hundreds."

We argue about that for several minutes—Carly and I say no, Matt says yes—until it's finally time for class.

Sure enough, Ms. McCoddle brings up the play as soon as we take our seats. She talks about what a great schoolwide event it will be while I draw ninjas in the margins of my notebook. (My favorite is a miniature ninja hiding behind a pair of salt and pepper shakers.)

Ms. McCoddle seems more relaxed than she was when Matt and I first had her in kindergarten; now she's one of the most respected teachers in our school.

"I'm not looking for someone who's directed a play before," Ms. McCoddle continues. "Just someone passionate about history."

respected

In the time it takes for me to draw a mustache on my ninja, Carly's raised her hand. Ms. McCoddle is used to Carly signing up for everything, so she scans the room first to make sure she's not leaving anybody out. But with Maria absent, Carly's the only one in class remotely interested in directing a history play and she gets the job.

passionate

Matt and I skateboard home after school and look up the martial arts school Carly found online.

"It seems too tame," Matt says.

tame

"I was hoping for something more ninja-y."

I click on some other schools that have classes in the area. "How about this one?"

Matt lets out a long whistle. "The Way of the Thunder Shadow. Now THAT'S what I'm talking about."

When Dad gets home, I ask if he can take us to check out the martial arts class tomorrow. He marks it on his phone calendar and says sure.

My dad's been much happier since he started working again. After being laid off from his job as a storyboard artist for almost a year, he finally started doing artwork for a guerrilla marketing company. At first I thought it was GORILLA marketing, which would be awesome,

guerrilla

especially if we could introduce our capuchin monkey, Frank, to a real gorilla. But it turns out my dad's company does groundbreaking advertising campaigns instead— much less fun than hanging out with gorillas.

groundbreaking

Matt and I search for the video controllers, which we finally find wedged between the cushions of the couch.

"You know it's a matter of time before Carly ropes us into helping her with that play."

Matt nods as he loads the latest version of Rayman. "We'll be too busy spying on people and practicing martial arts to help," he answers. "Real ninjas don't have time to paint scenery for a play."

scenery

He's right, but I also know Carly can be very persuasive. I hope this doesn't come down to choosing between two of my best friends.

The Dojo

Mom runs her veterinary practice from the office adjacent to our house, so that means there's always lots of people and their pets coming up and down the driveway. As Dad gets ready to drive Matt, Carly, and me to the martial arts studio, we're stopped by a woman walking a ferret on a leash.

The ferret wears a top hat and a tutu of colorful feathers. The poor

adjacent

ferret

plumage

animal looks like a Muppet with pink plumage.

"Please say Dr. Fallon can help Zippy with his stage fright. He's performing tonight and he's a wreck!" The woman coos and whispers to the ferret, who seems like he'd rather be anywhere else.

Dad assures her Mom has experience with lots of different animals and shows the woman to the office.

"You should totally get Frank a top hat," Matt says. "But definitely not a tutu."

"Frank needs a Lakers T-shirt," Carly says. "He watches more basketball on TV than I do."

My family and I are the foster home for Frank until he's old enough to go to Monkey College to learn to help people with physical disabilities do things like open doors, turn on lights, and fetch water bottles. Lately he's turned into a giant sports fan too, watching TV alongside me and my dog, Bodi.

fetch

I wanted Frank to wear one of those foam fingers they sell at games, but Mom was afraid he'd eat it. I fought her like crazy but she put her foot down. I guess it's a good thing she did because when I went to find the finger under my bed, Frank had already chewed it to a stub. Luckily he was okay; I on the other hand received yet another lecture on responsibility.

stub

We finally pile in the car and head to the martial arts studio. Because Carly wanted us to join the other studio in Santa Monica, she complains for a bit until we hit the highway. Umberto called the studio yesterday to see if they could accommodate him in a wheelchair but they said there would be a lot of kicking and mat work in class and he'd be better off studying with the instructor one-on-one. It's a shame because Umberto's the funniest kid I know and he'd be hilarious to have in class. Umberto said he didn't mind, but I wonder if that's true.

On the drive over, Carly talks about directing the play and Matt shoots me an I-Told-You-So face. We pretend to listen until Dad pulls into the parking lot of the dojo. He gets lots of texts at his new job— even on weekends—so he returns phone calls outside while the three of us go in.

The first person we see is a

twenty-something guy wearing a black gi who introduces himself as Dave. I try not to stare—the guy is lean and mean with a shaved head and pierced eyebrows. He might be the scariest guy I've ever seen in real life, so I'm surprised when his voice is quiet and I can barely hear him.

gi

pierced

"Welcome to the Way of the Thunder Shadow," he says. "A place where discipline and action unite."

The studio is dimly lit with black folding chairs in the waiting room. The walls are painted black with one wall of mirrors. Everything is black or red, except for the small fern withering in a pot by the door.

withering

"Do you have an appointment with Sensei Takai?" Dave asks.

I tell him we do and that we're interested in their Junior Ninja classes.

Dave slowly bows. "Sensei Takai will be with you soon."

The three of us sit in the darkened room and wait for what seems like an eternity. (Turns out, it was only about five minutes.)

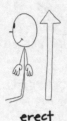

erect

An old man with the most erect posture I've ever seen enters the room quietly; Carly jumps out of her chair when she realizes he's standing beside her.

blurt

We wait for the sensei to speak but he just looks at us and smiles. After a few awkward minutes, I blurt out why we're here. "We want to be ninjas and we heard you're a great sensei."

The old man continues to stare

and smile while the three of us fidget.

The sensei wears a shinobi shozoku and head scarf covering everything except his eyes, and canvas tabi boots with split toes and rubber soles. All of his clothing is black. He looks like every ninja in every movie I've ever seen except he's old and standing perfectly still. We follow his lead and try to sit quietly.

Almost ten minutes later, he clears his throat to speak. His voice is even quieter than Dave's, so the three of us have to lean in to hear him.

"Welcome to my dojo," he says with a bow.

We made a list of several questions we wanted to ask but now the three of us just take turns looking at one another, not sure what to do next.

"Today's lesson is over," Sensei Takai says. "You practice until next time."

"Practice what?" Carly asks.

dismiss

Sensei Takai smiles, then waves his hand to dismiss us.

"But what are we supposed to do?" Carly asks again.

He bows one more time and leaves the room.

Carly spends most of her time trying to get everything just right, so an assignment with no instructions is unacceptable.

unacceptable

"It's obvious what we're supposed to do," Matt says when we're outside. "Right, Derek?"

I smirk like of course I know, but

I have absolutely no idea. Carly calls my bluff immediately.

"You guys are as clueless as I am, so stop pretending you're not!"

Matt and I finally admit we don't know what Sensei Takai expects us to practice.

"I didn't think being a ninja was going to be so complicated," Matt says. "I thought we could just act like spies."

I spot my dad at the coffee shop across the street. He waves and points to his phone, indicating he's almost finished with his call.

"The question is, are we coming back next week?" I ask my friends.

Carly shakes her head. "I hate not knowing what's expected of me."

"Welcome to my world," I say.

bluff

trickery

On the way home, Dad lets us stop for burgers and fries. Over our meal, we tell him about the session with Sensei Takai.

"Aren't ninjas trained in trickery?" Dad asks. "Maybe Sensei Takai is not telling you what to practice on purpose."

Matt, Carly, and I exchange glances. Have we just been tricked by a ninja?

A School Mystery

When we get to school on Monday, Mr. Demetri calls an emergency assembly. As we file in, the principal paces across the stage, impatiently waiting for us to take our seats. When he finally gets to the podium, he doesn't look happy.

impatiently

"There was an act of vandalism at the school this weekend. And you KNOW how I feel about vandalism."

podium

spree

Minotaur

tolerate

justice

He doesn't need to remind us how he reacts to destruction of school property. Last year some kids from the high school broke several windows on a crime spree and Mr. Demetri didn't rest until they were caught.

Mr. Demetri motions to Ms. Mateo, the assistant principal, and a slide fills the screen behind him. It's an illustration of a demented Minotaur that looks like it's spray-painted on the back of the school. A few kids start to laugh at the odd-looking creature but one look at our principal's face shuts them up fast.

"I will not tolerate this," Mr. Demetri continues. "Whoever is responsible will be brought to justice, mark my words."

Ms. Mateo gets up and makes a few announcements about the school play, mentioning there's a sign-up sheet outside the cafeteria. Carly beams when her name is mentioned as the director.

As we head back to class, Umberto skids his wheelchair, blocking our path. "You know what this whole vandalism thing means, don't you?"

"It means Mr. Demetri's going to want someone's head on a platter," Matt says.

But I know what Umberto's thinking because I'm thinking the same thing. "It means our school needs a hero."

"It means our school needs a spy," Matt says.

"I'm not sure I like where this is going," Carly says.

Matt, Umberto, and I say the next line in unison: "It means our school needs a NINJA!"

Using Our Spy Skills

Carly tries to get us to brainstorm ideas for the American Revolution play but Matt, Umberto, and I have bigger fish to fry.

We agree the first thing to do is examine the evidence. We head to the back of the school but Mr. Demetri has roped off the area with yellow caution tape.

"I feel like we're on the set of a crime show," I say. "It's not like someone was murdered here."

"Plus, that tape doesn't hide the graffiti." Umberto wheels his chair under the caution tape as if it's not even there.

sinister

The large Minotaur is drawn with dark purple paint. The bull's expression is sinister, with a toothy grin. The human body is muscular but his hands drag on the ground like an ape.

toothy

"Looks like the kind of thing *you* would draw," Matt says.

I shake my head in disagreement. "My version would be much more cartoony."

disagreement

Umberto backs up and studies the rest of the wall. "We should find out if other drawings were made around town or if this is the only one."

It's a shame Umberto can't join us for classes at the Way of the

Thunder Shadow because his ninja instincts are the best in the group.

We sit on one of the picnic tables behind the school and tell Umberto about Sensei Takai's silent treatment. Umberto acts like the whole routine makes perfect sense.

stealthy

"Ninjas have to be stealthy," he says. "And you can't be stealthy if you're not quiet. Ninjas are experts in silence."

"Who wants to be silent?" I ask.

Umberto smiles. "If you're not quiet, people can hear you coming. Plus, ninjas don't want anyone knowing who they are, so you have to be silent about that too."

"What good is being a ninja if you can't TELL anyone you're a ninja?" Matt asks. "This whole thing's starting to sound like a lot of work."

Umberto tells us Sensei Takai was probably forcing us to pay attention to what was around us. "We can practice silence now by studying the Minotaur drawing to see if we can learn anything."

It usually takes enormous concentration for me to keep quiet in school, and now I'm supposed to be quiet OUTSIDE of it too? But Umberto's focused on the Minotaur, as if some clue will suddenly burst out of its giant nostrils.

After a minute, I can't take it anymore and jump off the table. "There's something else ninjas have that we don't have—ninja clothes!"

Matt says he looked for some online but his mom said they were too expensive for what might turn out to be one of Matt's many short-lived hobbies.

short-lived

"My cousin has a white karate outfit I can borrow," Umberto says.

"I have lots of old gym clothes," Matt says. "But ninjas always wear black."

And just like that, I know what we're doing for the rest of the afternoon.

Paint It Black

The first thing I do when we get to my house is make sure Mom's in her office. We're in luck—the waiting room is full of people with dogs and cats, and with Dad at his new job, the coast is clear.

Matt stops at his house to gather extra sweatpants and shirts, which will soon be transformed into our awesome ninja outfits. Umberto has his video game design class, so

transformed

it's just Matt and me since Carly stayed after school to work on the play.

"I raided the box in the basement that my mom keeps for charity." Matt enters the kitchen with a giant handful of clothes. "She had liquid dye in the laundry room too."

charity

He tosses me a plastic bottle of dye and I scramble to catch it before it hits the floor. I stare at the white porcelain sink and ask Matt if the dye will stain it.

scramble

"Of course it'll stain—it's dye!"

I realize we need a Plan B so I go outside and rummage through the garage. In the corner, I find a big plastic tub full of old toys. Matt and I get sidetracked with some of my forgotten action figures, and before we know it, half an hour's gone by.

sidetracked

(I'm not sure real ninjas would get this distracted.)

I check on my mom one more time to make sure we're still safe. She's cleaning a German's shepherd's teeth and waves me off without looking up.

By the time I get back outside, Matt's dragged the plastic tub into the kitchen and is filling it with hot water from the sprayer. Maybe a real ninja would get towels but they're upstairs, so I grab an armload of newspapers from the recycling bin and place them around the floor instead.

"Remember that summer camp where we tie-dyed stuff all the time?" Matt asks.

"That counselor was definitely more focused on her boyfriend than crafts."

"I still remember how to do it." Matt begins wrapping rubber bands around one of the shirts.

"But that will make it tie-dyed!"

Matt shakes his head. "You need the rubber bands for the dye to work."

"No, the rubber bands will tie-dye it," I argue. "That's why they call it TIE-dye."

"Hey, who got all this stuff anyway?" Matt asks. "Believe it or not, I know what I'm doing."

Before I get a chance to look it up online, Matt is finished binding the clothes and thrusts them into the inky black water. I mope a little, thinking he's wrong, but I don't want to get into a fight with my best friend when he's so sure he's right.

mope

The instructions on the bottle

miraculously

say to stir the clothes in the hot water for thirty minutes, which seems like an awfully long time to stir anything. After ten minutes, we lift up one of the pieces, now miraculously black.

"I told you!" Matt says.

"They'll be tie-dyed after you take the bands off."

"No they won't." Matt brings the dripping clothes to the sink and undoes the bands.

starbursts

Sure enough, our new ninja outfits are covered in white starbursts.

"You might have been right about the bands," Matt says.

"MIGHT have been right? I was ABSOLUTELY right!"

We don't have time to argue because we both notice the clothes are not only tie-dyed but dripping all over the sink. And the floor.

Our hands are stained as black as the fabric.

"I guess we should've worn gloves," Matt says.

It's at this moment that my mom walks into the kitchen. The door hasn't even closed behind her before she starts dishing out a giant portion of MomMad.

"What are you doing?" she yells. "That's never going to come out!" She hurries to the sink and begins furiously scrubbing.

terrified

Matt and I stand there, too terrified to move. Mom hoses down the sink and wipes the floor, continuing her rant.

"You two should know better. Dye is permanent."

rant

I don't know about Matt but right now *I'M* the one who wants to permanently die.

Mom finally stops yelling and looks at the soggy tie-dyed clothes in the sink. "I'm guessing these were supposed to be ninja outfits?"

Matt and I nod morosely.

morosely

"I would've helped if you'd asked." She takes a wooden spoon and pokes at one of the shirts. "You do realize these are tie-dyed?"

Matt and I nod again and my mother laughs.

espionage

"I thought the big thing about ninjas was that no one saw them coming? I'm not sure how effective you'll be in the espionage department wearing these."

I know if I asked her, Mom would help us dye them the right way, but

I'm so glad she's not mad anymore that I keep my mouth shut. Matt and I finish wiping the floor, ruining the clothes we're wearing in the process.

"We still have a ways to go with this whole ninja thing," Matt says.

Which is all the more reason I'm looking forward to studying with Sensei Takai.

Did I just say I was looking forward to studying?

Our First Class

nunchucks

introduced

While Matt and I mess around with the bin of nunchucks, Carly's already introduced herself to half the people in class. She's her perky, friendly self and I can't help but smile at how easily she maneuvers through the world.

It turns out Sensei Takai only teaches a few kids at a time so we're lucky the three of us got in. The other kids look about our age:

two girls and one boy, all dressed in white gis. I can't speak for Matt, but I feel ridiculous in my tie-dyed outfit. Karen and Tanya look at me and giggle, as if they think I look bizarre too.

bizarre

Matt is oblivious to their jeers, hurling himself into the standing punching bag in the corner of the room. He stops when he spots Sensei Takai behind him. Nobody's better at sneaking up on you than our new teacher, except maybe Umberto.

chatty

Most of my teachers have been chatty—Ms. McCoddle especially—so it's a surprise to have someone in charge who stands there quietly. It doesn't take long for the six of us to line up and wait for instructions.

We wait.

And wait.

Matt whirls around to look at me with an expression as bewildered as mine. We both turn to Carly, who ignores us, staying focused on our teacher.

prolonged

After a prolonged silence, Sensei Takai bows. I'm not sure if we're supposed to bow back, but I follow along when the other kids do.

"Welcome," Sensei Takai finally says.

I wait for more words but none come.

Matt turns to me again and rolls his eyes. He doesn't need words for me to know what he's thinking: *Where's the action? The kicks? The spying?*

"Today we practice silence."

This time Matt's complaint is audible. "We did that last time! When are we going to do some martial arts?"

complaint

Sensei Takai smiles as if he's heard this question a thousand times. "This *is* martial arts," he says in a whisper. "Now silence."

Matt's not the only one confused; the rest of us spend more time looking at one another for guidance than we do following the teacher's instructions. When the girl in front of me starts to speak, Sensei Takai holds up his hand to stop her.

We spend the next thirty minutes staring at our teacher, not moving a muscle.

THIRTY MINUTES.

Finally Sensei Takai bows again, dismissing us without a sound.

"That was the worst class EVER," I blurt as soon as we get outside.

"I've been working so hard on the play, I think I actually slept standing up," Carly says.

decisively

"We need to find a new teacher," Matt says decisively. "This is *not* what I signed up for."

hobby

As we wait for Carly's mom to pick us up, I can't hide my disappointment. If you added up every hobby I've ever started then quit, the number would be gigantic. In fact, drawing and skateboarding are the only activities I've ever stuck with. Do I give up on things too soon?

Mrs. Rodriquez sees we're less than thrilled, so she asks if we want to stop for frozen yogurt. It's a nice offer that we gladly accept. But even as I swirl the Raspberry Delight into my cone, I can't help feeling that I've failed at something else yet again.

swirl

Another Crime

When I get to school on Monday, I don't need an assembly with Mr. Demetri to let me know something's wrong. The ten-foot-long Minotaur painted on the fence across from the school tells me our principal will be on the warpath.

stockade

The stockade fence belongs to a family who's as mad about the graffiti as Mr. Demetri. A group of us study the drawing as the buses unload.

Umberto skids over in his wheel-chair, breathless with the latest info.

breathless

"It's a guy and he almost got caught," he says. "If you look close, he didn't finish stenciling."

Sure enough, the Minotaur's foot drifts off the fence in what looks like a quick retreat.

stenciling

"We're not being good spies," Umberto continues. "*Real* ninjas would've had this solved by now."

He's right. We've been focusing on clothes and moves and making sure our scarves are right. A professional would've followed orders and gotten to the bottom of this already.

increase

I tell Umberto we need to increase our efforts; we'll round up Matt and Carly after school to look for new clues.

But Carly has different plans.

"You guys are helping me with the play this afternoon." She shuts her locker firmly as if we don't have a say in the matter.

Matt is the first to complain. "There's no way we're working on your play while there's a criminal on the loose!"

mocks

"What are you—a superhero?" Carly mocks. "Leave the sleuthing to the professionals—I need people to help me write some new scenes!"

sleuthing

Umberto slams his locker shut too. "We're never going to *be* professionals if we don't take this seriously." He turns to Matt and me. "Tie-dyed shinobi shozokus? Really?"

Umberto's always been more disciplined than Matt or me but I didn't realize he was this frustrated with our progress.

"We *can* solve this. We *should* solve this. We just have to stop fooling around!" Umberto continues.

His words pin Matt and me to our lockers.

"You're right," I finally say. "Let's get to the bottom of this."

Carly rolls her eyes; she's seen me promise to be more focused a thousand times before. "Does this mean you guys aren't going to help this afternoon?"

reprimand

But Umberto's reprimand has snapped me to attention. I tell Carly we'll solve the crime AND help her with the play.

She seems relieved and heads to class.

"You do this all the time," Matt

invincible

says. "Bite off more than you can chew. There's no way we can do both."

But somehow I feel invincible—at least until I get to math and there's a surprise quiz.

Ninja Night

Matt, Umberto, and I tell our parents we're meeting at the panini place near the school to work on a project. We DO eat dinner there, but as soon as we're done, we head to the school parking lot to try to catch the vandal in the act.

panini

"What are the chances the guy comes back to the same place?" Matt asks. "If I were him, I'd find a new spot to draw a Minotaur."

Umberto shakes his head. "He'll want to finish his drawing." He pulls out the notebook strapped to the back of his wheelchair. He flips through it until he finds the page he's looking for—a perfect duplicate of the Minotaur on the fence.

"Wait... YOU didn't draw the mural, did you?" I ask.

"Of course not!" Umberto says. "I just wanted to see if I could."

twinge

I examine the drawing, which is almost identical to the original. I feel a twinge of envy that Umberto's illustration skills have improved so much. He really is a much better cartoonist than I am.

He's also got this whole silence thing down. As we hide behind the bike rack, he has to tell Matt and me to keep it down several times. "Stop being so loud," he says. "It's very un-ninja."

improvise

But it's dark and we have the school parking lot to ourselves, so Matt and I improvise a hockey game with a flat rock. We take turns kicking it across the cement until Umberto waves his arms, wildly pointing to a car slowing down.

"Maybe one of our parents should've come with us," I whisper. "Maybe this mission is more dangerous than we thought." I reach into my pocket and take out my phone, just in case.

The car continues to head toward us, slowly.

"This could be the vandal," Matt whispers.

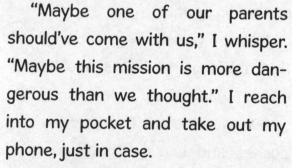

sedan

The sedan pulls over a few yards away from where we're hiding. I feel my pulse quicken; we're about to see who's behind this.

For several minutes, none of us move. Whoever's in the car remains as quiet as we are.

Suddenly, the door flies open and a man races toward us.

Matt, Umberto, and I look up to find our principal standing beside our hiding spot.

"Well! I was hoping whoever did this didn't go to this school, but I guess I was wrong."

stumble

We stumble out from behind the bushes and explain that we were trying to catch the vandal in the act too.

Mr. Demetri's not buying it. He spots Umberto's notebook and holds up the drawing of the Minotaur. "I'm so disappointed in you boys."

"We don't have any paint!" I say. "Look!"

Mr. Demetri searches through Umberto's pack and checks our bikes and wheelchair.

"We're ninjas!" Matt shouts, which doesn't make any sense.

Mr. Demetri is still suspicious and insists on taking us home. We squabble with him for several min- utes, explaining that Umberto's van driver is picking him up at the panini place in ten minutes, which is true.

squabble

Our principal looks at us with a steely glare. "I'm calling all your par- ents tonight."

We protest even louder.

steely

"I've got my eyes on you three. And after I'm done with my phone calls, your parents will have their eyes on you too."

All I want is for this night to end. Mr. Demetri follows behind us in his car as we head back to the restaurant.

"We were just trying to help!" I whisper. "Now we're his top suspects!"

"And he's calling our parents!" Matt adds. "My mom's gonna kill me."

"We're the worst ninjas ever," Umberto says.

Which is totally, completely true.

Carly's Play

My parents are NOT happy after Mr. Demetri's phone call and we have a long "chat" about how I left out a few key facts when I told them Matt, Umberto, and I were going to the panini place. Luckily they believe me when I say we aren't involved with the vandalism. Dad tells me not to stick my nose where it doesn't belong.

The next day I go out of my way

to avoid Mr. Demetri, even volunteering to help Carly with her play so I don't have to see him in the hall.

Carly tells us she spent several hours in the media center doing research and came to the conclusion there weren't enough stories about girls in the history textbooks. She

scrapped

scrapped the original idea for the play and Ms. McCoddle gave her blessing for Carly to write her own. Now Carly's got a ton of work to do before the show.

direction

"I know you guys aren't good at taking direction," Carly begins, "but do you think for once, *I* can be in charge?"

I'm pretty sure Matt and Umberto are thinking the same two words as I am—FAT CHANCE—but the three of us smile and tell Carly we're happy to let her be the boss this time.

At rehearsal, she doesn't waste a minute, calling out orders faster than a drill sergeant. We hurry around the auditorium, moving plywood and laying down drop cloths, telling anyone within earshot about our run-in with Mr. Demetri. Whoever's behind the Minotaur has the whole school buzzing.

earshot

Carly introduces us to two new girls—Darcy and Farida. Darcy transferred from another school in L.A. and Farida just moved here from the Middle East. When I start talking to her in a slow, loud voice, Carly elbows me and says Farida speaks perfect English.

Farida giggles and I notice she has the longest eyelashes I've ever

feisty

seen. Darcy is loud and feisty, pushing Umberto up and down the aisles of the auditorium. They whizz by so fast, I can't tell if the expression on his face is one of fear or glee.

As usual, Carly has every detail covered, from the scenery to the lighting to the costumes and casting.

"This is the first time the school's done a play focusing on the role girls had in the Revolution. Ms. McCoddle said it was an innovative idea."

As she talks, I visualize one of my old vocabulary notebooks, trying to remember the drawing I did for the word *innovative*. I finally picture it: a guy who looks like Thomas Edison holding a lightbulb with another one flickering over his head. I guess what

flickering

Carly's saying is that telling the girls' story is a bright idea.

"We're doing scenes from the Battles of Lexington and Concord," Carly says. "So the scenery needs to be trees, fences, and stone walls."

Matt, Farida, and I open several jars of paint while Darcy and Umberto go to the media center to bring back photographs we can copy.

supervisor

Carly's very comfortable in the role of supervisor, crossing out tasks from her to-do list as soon as they're completed.

It's been a few months since Carly and I shared an awkward kiss at my house, and neither of us wants to be the first to bring it up. I've gone out of my way NOT to be alone with her to make sure that conversation never happens. But as I help her get more paintbrushes, I realize we're the only ones in the art room.

Suppose she says something? Suppose I have to say something back?

Thankfully Matt and Umberto save me from my own thoughts by bursting into the room.

"The guy came back to finish the drawing!" Umberto cries. "I told you he would!"

We race toward the entrance of the school. The others are excited to look for clues, but all I'm thinking is that Minotaur guy got me out of an uncomfortable imaginary conversation with Carly.

I just hope my head is where that conversation stays.

Umberto Saves
the Day

We're only a few feet down the hall before we run into Mr. Demetri. He's standing by our lockers, gesturing for us to approach.

gesturing

"Just the students I'm looking for." He points to Matt, Umberto, then me.

"It wasn't us!" I cry.

The principal ushers the three of us into his office, leaving Carly stranded in the hall alone.

stranded

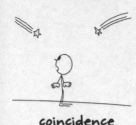

coincidence

proclaim

innocence

Matt and Umberto look as fearful as I am when Mr. Demetri shuts the door behind us.

"Are you trying to tell me it's a coincidence that I saw the three of you here last night and today there's *more* vandalism? In the exact same place?"

"You saw us leave!" Matt says.

"You could have come back," Mr. Demetri says.

"You talked to our parents," Umberto adds.

Umberto, Matt, and I continue to proclaim our innocence but Mr. Demetri's not buying it. Before he can grab the directory of home addresses and phone numbers from the shelf, Umberto wheels himself over to Mr. Demetri. He doesn't speak, just calmly stares the principal down. After a few moments, Mr. Demetri puts away the directory.

When Umberto does speak, his voice is calm and soothing. "Why would we return to the scene of the crime after you saw us there? That doesn't make sense."

soothing

Matt's about to chime in, but I motion for him to keep quiet. Umberto has this covered.

"Besides," Umberto continues, "we like this school. Why would we deface it?"

deface

The calmness of Umberto's voice seems to hypnotize Mr. Demetri. The principal sits back in his chair and stares out the window.

"I wish I knew why someone was

hypnotize

doing this," Mr. Demetri finally says. "This whole mess is taking up too much of my time."

"Time that could be spent on the school play." Matt points to the poster hanging on Mr. Demetri's bulletin board. "It's going to be a great event."

Matt is totally kissing the principal's butt and it seems to be working. As he stares out the window, Mr. Demetri tells us to go back to class.

"That was amazing," I tell Umberto when we're in the hall. "You totally saved us."

Umberto smiles slow and wide like the Cheshire cat. "The best ninjas know that sometimes you need to be quiet to prevail."

Being quiet has never been easy,

prevail

but I can certainly see the plus side of it now. He might not be able to attend the classes, but Umberto is the real sensei in our group, hands down.

Frank and Bodi

thrilling

The rest of the school day is boring compared to the excitement of being called into the principal's office. Even a bird flying into Ms. Miller's classroom isn't as thrilling as it would've been before. Whoever is behind drawing the Minotaurs sure has taken the school by storm.

When I get back home, Bodi almost knocks me over. Between school and practicing my ninja moves,

I've barely had time to walk him lately.

Bodi's getting older but some-times he musters his old puppy energy and today is one of those days. He circles around me several times as I grab a stalk of celery from the fridge and plunge it into the jar of peanut butter. By the time Bodi finally settles down, I've gone through the entire bag of celery.

plunge

Sooner or later, Frank's going to have to go back to the organization that will train him to work with the disabled. Still, I keep hoping they'll forget he's here and Frank can stay with us forever.

The second I unlock his cage, he leaps out of captivity, straight onto my shoulder.

captivity

regimen

I know we're only supposed to be getting Frank used to living with humans but I've begun his training regimen anyway. I've taught him how to turn on the TV and the light switch in the living room. I've given up trying to talk Umberto into letting Frank help him around his house; even with the offer of a monkey helper, Umberto insists on doing everything himself.

When we first got Frank, Mom wouldn't let me take him out of the house, but over time, she relented and now he gets to accompany me around the neighborhood.

I used to feel stupid carrying a monkey around in a baby Snugli attached to my chest but both Mom and Frank's organization insisted. I'm just happy to be able to take Frank outside now without him climbing to the top of a tree.

On the way to the park, I pass a fire hydrant spraying water all over the street. It looks like someone popped the nozzle off the top of it with a crowbar. Considering we've been in a drought for years, it's a real shame. I look around to find the culprit but don't see anyone. All Bodi wants to do is lap up the puddles while Frank squirms to get out of the Snugli. I pet the top of my monkey's head until he finally calms down.

This new act of vandalism gets me thinking about the Minotaur graffiti. I have to admit it was funny and cool in the beginning, but as time

hydrant

nozzle

culprit

administrators

custodian

curse

goes on, I can see how Mr. Demetri and the other administrators are annoyed. Is the person behind the mysterious artwork trying to express himself or make people angry? Mr. Costanzo, our custodian, certainly was mad; Matt and I couldn't help laughing as Mr. Costanzo scrubbed the paint off the back of the school. We weren't laughing at his hard work but at the curse words he muttered under his breath when he couldn't remove the paint.

I let Bodi off the leash at the dog park and, as usual, Frank wants to be set free too. As much as I'd like to, I know from experience how hard it will be to get him back in the Snugli.

Mrs. Garfield throws a ball to Trixie, her golden retriever, then sees me and waves. I'm glad the days of having to explain why I'm carrying a capuchin in a baby carrier are over.

I sit on the bench as Bodi sniffs his way around the park. There's no ninja class tomorrow, so Matt, Carly, and I have the rest of the week to decide if we're quitting Sensei Takai's class. Standing in silence for half an hour was torture but I have to admit that watching Umberto with Mr. Demetri makes me think twice about the power of silence. Maybe Sensei Takai has something to teach us after all.

By the time Bodi's ready to head home, I make a decision. No matter what Matt and Carly decide, I'm going to give Sensei Takai one more chance.

Saturday with Dad

tranquilizer

subdue

malnourished

Because Mom has experience working with exotic animals, she sometimes gets called in to help with strange situations. Yesterday a mountain lion was spotted roaming through Griffith Park and the rangers had to shoot him with their tranquilizer guns to subdue him. It turns out he was malnourished, which was why he was wandering so close to humans. The animal sanctuary they brought him to contacted Mom, so she's spending the day caring for a hungry mountain lion. It seems like an unsafe activity for a Saturday, but she's excited by the prospect of helping an animal in need.

While Mom's doing that, Dad drags me on a bunch of errands. Some of them are lame (dry cleaners, shoe repair) but some of them are cool (phone store). My favorite is the superstore he goes to once a month to stock up on giant bottles of mayonnaise and detergent. We can easily spend a few hours here; Dad looks at printers while I roam the aisles for free food.

detergent

There's a woman handing out samples of chocolate-covered pretzels in tiny paper cups in the corner of the store. I come back every few minutes but she catches on after the fourth time and shoots me a look to get lost.

appliance

The checkout line is the longest I've ever seen, snaking from the front of the store to the appliance department. Dad tries to engage me in a game of I Spy while we wait, but that hasn't worked since I was little, so I hit up the sample tables one more time, leaving him to wait in line alone.

Back home, we put the groceries away and Dad challenges me to a video game. One fun result of Dad getting laid off last year was that he and I discovered we liked playing video games together. Most of the time I beat him, but once in a while he surprises me and kicks my butt. We play for an hour, eating in front of the TV, which Mom usually doesn't like us to do.

When I look for him later to tell him I'm skateboarding over to Matt's, I find him at his desk, buried under a stack of portfolios.

"Before you leave, would you mind sharing some of your art expertise?" he asks.

expertise

It's nice of Dad to ask for my help but he knows a thousand times more about art than I ever will. I do appreciate the way he always tries to make me feel like my opinion is valuable.

valuable

He flips through the large leather folder and shows me several illustrations. Some are busy and colorful; others are more traditional. Dad sorts them into several different piles across his desk.

traditional

"We're looking to bring on a few more artists for this new advertising campaign. I'm setting up interviews now—which of these artists would *you* bring in?"

I look through the various drawings while Dad tells me about the different artists—one a graduate

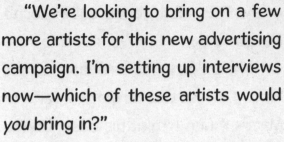

graduate

student at USC, another a web designer in Pasadena.

"The ones in this pile are funny," I tell him. "And the writing is so fancy."

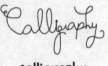

calligraphy

He tells me it's called calligraphy. I look at the drawings again and tell him I like them the best.

"That's what I think too." He tells me he'll set up an appointment with Felix Manning.

"If he's half as funny as his name, he'll definitely do a cool campaign."

Just as I'm about to head to Matt's, my mother pulls into the driveway. She's overflowing with stories about how she tried to feed a sick mountain lion pieces of meat. By the time she's finished, it's too late to go to Matt's.

overflowing

But I don't mind—it's not every day you get to hear your mom talk about tangling with a dangerous predator.

predator

You Want Us to What?

Umberto, Matt, and I have been putting off Carly for a week and I'm starting to feel guilty. She's one of our best friends and I think we should help her, but let's face it—there are a billion other things we'd rather do in our time off from school. Carly's persistent and finally pins us down to meet her in the auditorium after school.

persistent

"Okay, listen up!" Carly's tone is

all business as we settle down. "We need more actors in some key roles, so I'm hoping a few of you will volunteer."

In the back of the room, Matt, Umberto, and I are only half listening because we're taking turns playing a new game on Matt's phone. (Let me just say it shouldn't be so hard to flip a pancake.)

"I'm happy with the parts we've already cast," Carly continues. "But we can't have a play about our country's fight for independence without Paul Revere."

independence

"Paul Revere was a tattletale!" Darcy says.

Umberto snaps his head with a start. "I'LL be Paul Revere!"

tattletale

In all the time I've known Umberto, I've never heard him

wisecracking

animated

mention acting once. But the thought of a wisecracking, multiracial Paul Revere in a wheelchair brings a giant smile to my face.

"Done!" Carly says. "Now I need someone to play Sybil Ludington."

"Who's Sybil Ludington?" Darcy asks. "Is that a boy or a girl?"

Carly gets animated as she shares information she has learned about female war heroes. "Sybil Ludington's ride was more than twice as long as Paul Revere's, plus it was through the night—alone. And she was only sixteen!"

Darcy waves her hand. "I'll be Sybil Ludington. She sounds awesome!"

Matt pretends he's reaching for the phone but elbows me instead. "I bet you a dollar Umberto and Darcy are going out by the end of this play. You in?"

I can't tell if Umberto and Darcy are flirting with each other or just kidding around. Will all my friends have girlfriends soon? Did I miss the boat with the whole kissing-Carly thing? And most important, should I take this bet with Matt? These are the things I wonder about while Carly continues to cast the play.

flirting

identified

"I really identified with Abigail Adams," Carly says, "so I'm happy to play her if no one else wants to." Carly looks around to see if anyone cares but no one does. "John Adams played a key role in the Revolution—who wants to play him?"

"Derek!" Matt shouts.

"What?!" I say.

"He's been talking about it all week," Matt continues.

"I have not!"

agitated

I look over at Matt; I've seen this smirk on his face a million times before. He's doing this to get me agitated so he can laugh when I freak out. But I'm not going to.

"I'd love to play John Adams," I say. "He was a great guy." I pray no one in the group asks me for details because I don't know more than a few basic facts.

duress

"Are you sure you want to?" Carly asks. "I'd hate to see anyone take a part under duress."

I tell Carly I'm happy to join the cast. If only she knew I just accepted Matt's challenge as a way to shut him up.

Sensei's Lesson

Carly bowed out of class with Sensei Takai to visit her friend Amanda in San Diego. I like Amanda and always look forward to seeing her when she comes to L.A. I'm sure the two of them will have a blast, but it's the first time I've seen Carly give up on a challenge so quickly.

Even without a fun weekend in San Diego, I can't say I'm surprised Carly's disheartened with Sensei

disheartened

Takai's class. On the drive today, Matt and I talk about what we'll do if our teacher asks us to just stand there again.

"It's like that movie *The Karate Kid*," Dad jokes. "Wax on, wax off."

Neither Matt nor I have seen the movie, so my father has to explain. "The main character wants to learn karate and—like you two—all he wants to study are kicks and punches. But his sensei makes him do things like wax his car and paint his house. The kid gets really frustrated but all the while the exercises are strengthening the boy's skills—mentally and physically."

strengthening

"Are you telling us Sensei Takai is copying some lame movie?" I ask. "He's supposed to be an expert!"

"Maybe the teacher in the movie

was based on an expert too," Dad says. "Who knows? Maybe students have been studying this way for thousands of years."

"I am NOT painting Sensei Takai's house," Matt says.

"Or garage," I add.

"Or doghouse."

"Or fence."

Dad laughs as he pulls into the parking lot. "Maybe you two should spend a little more time thinking about what you WILL do instead of what you won't."

He tells us he'll be at the coffee shop where he's set up interviews. At least Dad will have a productive day while Matt and I stare into space.

productive

When class begins, Sensei Takai whispers hello from the back of the

composure

room. How is it possible for someone this old to sneak up on five kids? The girl next to me actually screams.

"Must regain composure," he says. "Time to settle down."

I figure he wants us to sit, but as soon as I start to, Sensei Takai motions for me to stand back up.

"Today we stand."

Matt pipes up immediately. "We stood *last* time!"

"Today we stand on one foot." Sensei Takai tucks his right foot against his left. He looks as sturdy as an oak tree.

balance

I, on the other hand, wobble and almost fall a dozen times.

"You need balance," our teacher says. "Not just in martial arts but in all things."

The girl Sensei Takai startled is as off balance as I am. She keeps falling over, and when she finally does stand, the leg with her weight trembles. Matt shoots me a look that tells me today is DEFINITELY his last class. I'm just glad our teacher's not making us wax his car like that guy in the movie.

trembles

After an excruciating twenty minutes, Sensei Takai stands on both feet as if standing on one leg for that long was the easiest thing in the world. (The girl next to me moans and rubs her foot like she just scaled Mount Everest. So dramatic.)

scaled

"Tonight's homework—" the teacher begins.

"HOMEWORK?!" Matt and I shout.

Sensei Takai can't help but smile.

"Tonight's homework is to stand on one foot every day for as long as you can until our next class."

"Which is going to be never," Matt whispers as we head to the door.

"Do you think we were doing it right?" I ask.

"You sound like Carly," Matt says. "This is what happens when you start pretending to be her husband in a play."

I stop short in front of the door. "I'm not her HUSBAND—I'm John Adams. Future president, I might add."

"Yes, and she's ABIGAIL Adams—your wife!"

Even on this chilly afternoon, I feel my cheeks flush. "Why didn't you tell me that?"

Matt laughs. "Why didn't you listen?"

This whole thing reminds me of Susie trying to talk Calvin into playing house with her in one of my favorite *Calvin and Hobbes* strips. In other words, not good.

At the coffee shop, Dad introduces us to Felix, who he just hired. The guy has big black glasses and is loading up a leather saddlebag with his artwork. When Dad asks if we want hot chocolates, we happily take him up on the offer.

saddlebag

Both Felix and Dad laugh when they hear we just spent half the class standing on one foot.

"It's building your balance and your discipline," Dad says. "But for fifty bucks a class, you can stand on one leg at home."

"Sounds like you guys aren't enjoying your ninternship as much as you thought," Felix adds.

We laugh at the joke, tell Felix it was nice to meet him, then head home. As we get closer to our neighborhood, we spot two police cars in front of the high school.

"What happened here?" Dad asks.

crane

One of the officers waves us past as Matt and I crane our necks to see what's going on.

The front of the high school is covered with a Minotaur mural.

Things Get Serious

Here are the facts:

mythological

- There are three murals around town featuring the mythological beast.
- They've all been created at night.
- They're all only about four feet tall but more than eight feet in length.

- They use the same colors: purple, lime green, black, and yellow.
- No one has any idea who's behind it, including Mr. Demetri and the police.

"Don't you think it's weird the murals are all so low?" Matt asks. "If I were the artist, I'd use the whole wall."

troll

"And why a Minotaur?" I wonder. "Is there a reason the vandal picked that and not a troll? Or a toothbrush?"

toothbrush

"The vandal's got to be over eighteen," Matt continues. "Do you know how hard it is to buy cans of spray paint in this city? When I was doing my project for the science fair, Jamie had to show his ID at the hardware store before they'd sell me any."

It's true—or at least that's what my dad said last night as we drove through the police blockade. He said the city passed a law a few years ago to cut off access to spray paint as the first step in cracking down on the city's rampant graffiti.

blockade

access

"The Minotaur guy could have his older brother buying paint for him, just like Jamie did for you. Either way, he's certainly putting in a lot of effort."

Obviously, Mr. Demetri is working on this 24/7. We didn't have an assembly this time, but he certainly has a lot to say during the morning announcement. After a while it sounds like the grown-ups in a

trombone

Charlie Brown cartoon—all I can hear is a trombone *MWA MWA MWA*. (As someone interested in solving the case, I guess I should be paying closer attention....)

On our way to English, Carly reminds us we have rehearsal after school today. I hate to say it but that kind of sounds like *MWA MWA MWA* too.

Matt elbows me when he spots Umberto heading down the hall with Darcy. "You owe me money," Matt says. "I told you this would happen."

But I'm not looking at Umberto and Darcy laughing and talking as they pass the lockers. My eyes are glued on the nylon pack that's always affixed to Umberto's chair. Since I've known him, that pack's

affixed

been stuffed with books, maga-
zines, art projects, lunch bags, and
baseball hats. I've never before seen
what's tucked inside Umberto's pack
today.

A can of purple spray paint.

Rehearsal

"You're seeing things," Matt says after I share what I saw. "There's no way Umberto's the vandal."

I tell him I'm not saying Umberto IS the guy behind the Minotaur, I'm just saying he had a can of spray paint in his pack.

"Purple *is* one of the colors," Matt says. "And Umberto *did* have a perfect copy of the drawing in his sketchbook the other day."

"The murals are all low to the ground—someone COULD create them sitting down."

We get the same idea at the same time—to go to the high school and look for wheel tracks. But even as we make the plan for after rehearsal, I'm already second-guessing myself.

"Umberto's our friend," I begin. "Not some random lawbreaker."

lawbreaker

"He *is* our friend," Matt says. "But remember how it was when we first met him?"

Matt doesn't need to remind me how Umberto and I clashed when he transferred to our school. Sure, he made my life miserable but that doesn't make him a criminal.

clashed

Matt and I decide to be vigilant and keep our eyes on Umberto while

hardware

looking for clues that might point to someone else. But for the rest of the day, all I can do is wonder about one of my best friends. Why did Umberto have that paint—especially if hardware stores can't sell cans to anyone under eighteen? And why take the time to draw a perfect Minotaur in his notebook? I'm an artist too, but I didn't try to copy it.

Now that I think of it, Umberto told Matt and me not to bother to wait for his van driver that night when Mr. Demetri caught us at school. Maybe Bill never came to pick him up; maybe Umberto went back to the scene of the crime after Matt and I left.

I barely listen in my classes because my mind is focused on one thing—could Umberto have a secret life?

Carly makes sure Matt, Umberto, and I show up at rehearsal by telling us she made homemade chocolate chip brownies for the occasion. I'm not sure Umberto needs the extra motivation, because when Matt and I get there, Umberto and Darcy are already running their lines. It might not make sense, but Matt and I take this as a sign that we should have two brownies instead of one. (I said it might not make sense.)

Carly is handing out a schedule of the scenes we'll be rehearsing. Umberto zooms by as Paul Revere in a wheelchair and I try to catch a glimpse of his pack.

His sketchbook is there but the

occasion

motivation

schedule

can of spray paint is gone. Matt pulls me aside after Umberto passes by.

"Either he knows we're onto him and hid the evidence or you just THOUGHT you saw a can of paint."

I assure Matt that there definitely was a paint can in Umberto's pack.

"You guys want to get some pizza after rehearsal?" Umberto wheels over during a break. "Bill can't pick me up for a while so there'll be time."

flimsy

I stammer out an excuse about homework, which sounds flimsy even to me. Should Matt and I level with Umberto and ask him about the paint instead of lying to our friend?

"What were we supposed to say?" Matt asks me later. "'Do you want to come with us to the high school and look for tire prints from your wheelchair?' Come on, we HAD to lie!"

I think about Sensei Takai and his lessons of discipline and balance. It feels wrong to lie to Umberto. On the other hand, ninjas are experts at deception and Umberto is the best ninja in our group. Has he been deceiving Matt, Carly, and me this whole time?

deception

Ninja Stars

Doug and Farida's scene takes so long to rehearse that Carly and I don't get a chance to practice ours. On the way out, Carly asks if I want to come over and run through the scene at her house later. The web of lies continues as I tell Carly I just made plans with Matt to skateboard.

"You know how people say it gets easier to lie the more you do it?" I ask Matt. "I think that's true." I feel horrible lying to two of our best friends within minutes of each other, but I know Carly wouldn't approve of our plan to check out the high school mural.

"It's not lying if we skateboard there," Matt answers.

We jump on our boards and head to the high school. I've been here for a fundraiser for animal rights with my mom but don't remember the school's layout. Because he has an older brother, Matt knows the high school, but he's as surprised as I am when we reach the front.

fundraiser

layout

The entire building is surrounded by a three-foot cement border.

"There's no way we'll see tire prints here," Matt says.

"Or footprints—I'm still hoping it's NOT Umberto."

"Of course it's not Umberto—we're being ridiculous. Maybe it's so low because the vandal is from the elementary school," Matt suggests.

"Or a Mommy-and-me playgroup," I add. "Where the moms buy paint for the toddlers."

leprechaun

"Or maybe a leprechaun," Matt continues, "and there's a pot of gold around here."

As we skateboard, we recite more silly examples—circus performers, bent-over grandmas—until we get to my house. I'm surprised to find a strange guy sitting in our kitchen eating a bowl of soup. I'm about to run out the door, when he introduces himself as Charlie, Mom's new vet tech. I must look skeptical because he shows me his ID on a lanyard.

"The microwave in the office is broken," Charlie explains. "Your mom said I could use the one in the house."

I tell him it's no problem but wince when he slurps his soup noisily.

wince

"Your mom said you like to draw," Charlie says. "I draw too." He pulls out a small lined notebook from the pocket of his scrubs. Inside is a picture of a dog with rotting teeth. Charlie tells us he sketched this last week while my mom was working on the German shepherd.

slurps

When he finally leaves, Matt and I grab some lemon cookies Mom baked and I ask Matt if he wants to practice our standing-on-one-leg homework for Sensei Takai's class.

flamingo

"We were supposed to learn kicks and throw ninja stars," he says. "Not stand on one leg like a flamingo."

I take a bite out of my lemon cookie, turn it, and take another bite. Matt immediately knows what I'm going for and bites his cookie around the edges too. Soon we have a pile of cookie ninja stars.

"Inside or outside?" Matt asks.

"My mom's already going to be mad we ate all the cookies—let's at least throw them outside so she doesn't go ballistic."

Matt and I hold our shirts out and fill the pouches with stars. The next half hour is spent hurling lemon ninja stars at each other.

I'd like to say we don't eat the cookies off the ground when we're done, but we do.

Rehearsing with Carly

Mom can't stop talking about Charlie at dinner. I guess when he's not drawing pictures of dogs with rotten teeth, he's helping her streamline things around the office.

streamline

"Maybe he can fix the microwave so he doesn't have to slurp his soup in the house," I suggest.

She tells me Dad's picking up a new microwave on his way home from work. He's been working longer hours with his company's new advertising campaign but he seems to like it, which is good. I can't imagine working so hard and NOT liking what you do.

When I tell Mom I'm going over to Carly's to rehearse for the school play, she tells me to take Maria, Carly's mother, some of the lemon cookies. She opens the plastic container on the counter and finds only crumbs.

container

She looks at me with the same exasperated face I've seen a billion times. I mumble, "Sorry," and head over to Carly's.

Carly opens the door wearing a dress with an old-fashioned petticoat. On her head is a starched white bonnet.

petticoat

"I didn't realize this was a DRESS

rehearsal!" I haven't stepped into the house yet and I already feel like an amateur. I tried to learn my lines before dinner but couldn't get further than the first paragraph.

Carly seems embarrassed she's overdressed for the occasion and pulls the bonnet off. "I wanted to try it on to see if it fits. You don't have to make a big deal out of it."

I feel like I did something wrong but I'm not sure what it is. Luckily Mrs. Rodriquez comes in and diffuses the tension. We talk about the play and how hard Carly's been working to create something original. After a few minutes, Carly and I head downstairs.

original

When she talks about our scene, her voice is softer than usual, noticeably different from the teacher voice she uses at school. It hits me that this is the first time Carly and I have been alone since that day in the art room the other week when my imagination went wild. If tonight gets weird, maybe I can pretend to come down with asthma and leave. I'm not sure that's even possible but I might have to go with it if things get awkward.

asthma

"Abigail Adams was an amazing woman," Carly begins. "She and John Adams weren't just husband and wife; they were political partners, which was unusual for the time."

I already don't like where this one-sided conversation is headed.

"Abigail loved to read and studied lots of different subjects."

"Sounds like you." I search the

room to see if there are any cookies or treats down here and am excited when I spot a bowl of mini candy bars probably left over from Halloween.

"Abigail was married to the second president of the United States and was the mother of the sixth."

"John Quincy Adams, right?"

"Exactly." Carly sits next to me on the couch and holds out her hand for one of the candies.

I give her an almond bar, then grab the bonnet from the table and put it on. "Let's get started, shall we?" I say in a girly voice.

Carly laughs and we each take out our scripts. She's so orderly, she's highlighted all the parts for every member of the cast in different colors. I doubt highlighters were

orderly

invented in the 1700s, but it sounds like Abigail Adams would've used them if they were.

"Abigail and John Adams wrote over eleven hundred letters to each other—do you believe it?" Carly asks.

"Eleven hundred? Too bad they couldn't just text."

Carly rolls her eyes. "Their letters were amazing. We'll be sitting at two desks onstage reading from them."

dialogue

"Wait? What?" I flip through the pages of my script. I'd been paying attention to the dialogue and never read the stage directions. "Umberto gets to zoom around in his wheelchair as Paul Revere and I have to sit at a desk? I sit at a desk enough at school!"

"It'll be dramatic," Carly says. "Their letters were very powerful."

All the gears in my brain grind to a halt. "Are we talking about LOVE letters?"

Carly turns away when she answers. "They were apart from each other a lot, so some of them are."

I feel like I just got hit in the head with a mallet. "You can't possibly think I'm going to sit onstage and read you love letters!"

From the tone of her voice I can tell she's starting to get mad. "Not TO me. WITH me."

"Isn't that the same thing?"

"This was a stupid idea!" Carly says. "I KNEW you didn't want to be in the play! Matt just goaded you on!"

goaded

I have no idea what the word *goaded* means but I think I know what she's trying to say. "You should look for another John Adams to read love letters to because I quit!" I yank the bonnet off my head and storm upstairs.

fuming

On my way out, I act nice to Mrs. Rodriquez even though I'm fuming. Carly and I have had our disagreements before, but this feels like one of the worst.

Did all this anger and weirdness stem from that stupid kiss? If it did, I'd give anything for a time machine to travel back and erase that moment forever.

Someone New to Spy On

The people in Mom's office are having a party for her birthday to-morrow with some snacks and a cake. Charlie came over—thankfully not to eat soup—to invite Dad and me. Dad says he'll leave work early to attend.

Neither of my parents likes going anywhere empty-handed, so Dad sends me to the market the next day to pick up a platter of crudités

crudités

aimlessly

mascots

to bring to the party. I wander around the store aimlessly, trying to figure out what I'm supposed to get, until a helpful clerk tells me crudités means cut-up carrots and celery. Why didn't Dad just say that?

While I wait for the woman behind the deli counter to assemble the vegetables on a platter, I roam around the aisles. The rows of cereal are the most fun; I pretend the different cartoon mascots come to life and take over the store. The woman at the end of the aisle stares as I make explosion noises and tumble across the floor. Unfortunately, I misjudge the distance and end up knocking over a display of toilet paper. I lie there hoping the other shoppers will think the toilet paper spontaneously fell.

Three people are waiting in the checkout line, all staring.

One of them is Sensei Takai.

I do a double-take because I've never seen our teacher in regular clothes, never mind grocery shopping. He's wearing a cardigan sweater and khaki pants—just a regular old man buying apple juice and cough drops. (I looked in his basket.)

cardigan

double-take

I've seen disappointment on my parents' faces a million times before, but having your sensei find you in a giant pile of toilet paper is a whole new level of humiliation.

I'm suddenly horrified by my antics and scramble out of the mess I've just created.

antics

Sensei Takai still hasn't said a word.

I don't want to get reprimanded

by the manager to pick up the toilet paper so I rush to put the packages back.

"Out getting some groceries, huh?" I ask Sensei Takai. "I'm getting some crudités."

The other customers look on as I continue to babble.

"Crudités means cut-up vegetables. Crazy, right? Such a fancy word for something so simple. My mom's employees are throwing a party for her birthday. She's a veterinarian— funny place for a party, right?"

The store manager leaves once he sees the display's back in order. I'm desperate for my sensei to say ANYTHING but he just looks at me blankly, which is the biggest punishment of all.

Sensei Takai places his basket in

front of the cashier. The woman from the deli counter approaches with the platter of appetizers. I thank her and head to one of the other lines; the last thing I want is to stand behind Sensei Takai.

cashier

I'm the worst ninja ever.

My First Office Party

To say my chance meeting with Sensei Takai ruined the afternoon is an understatement. How am I supposed to have fun at a party when I feel like a three-year-old who just got caught with his hand in the cookie jar? Thankfully Matt stops over to wish Mom a happy birthday, so I have someone I can tell the whole embarrassing story to.

Matt laughs at the image of me

in a toilet paper landslide but most of his questions are about Sensei Takai. He wants to know what he wore, who he was with, if you could tell he was a martial arts master by the way he moved.

landslide

"He just looked like a regular man," I answer. "Maybe he's not some famous ninja warrior after all."

"That whole silent thing drives me crazy," Matt adds. "I wish the guy would just yell like a normal person."

"Or fart," I say.

"Or burp," Matt says.

"Or puke." And just like that I'm regular old Derek again. I guess that's the best thing a friend can do—get you back to feeling like yourself during those times when you don't.

buffoon

concocted

decorations

But I can't stop picturing Sensei Takai's face as he watched me make a mess in the grocery store. He didn't HAVE to say anything—his stare was enough to let me know I was acting like a buffoon. Even though I goof around with Matt and my dad at the party, I feel a little disappointed in myself too. I know Matt's bored with Sensei Takai's methods but today's disaster makes me feel I need to learn what our sensei has to teach even more.

My mom's office manager concocted a story about a new printing system to get Mom out of the office while the rest of the staff sets up the party. Matt, Dad, and I help Charlie fill the waiting room with decorations— red balloons with paw prints and strings of dog bones. Nancy, the receptionist, places a dark-choco-late-and-vanilla cake on the table. It's in the shape of a dalmatian and Matt and I have to control ourselves not to dig in before Mom arrives.

"Good job not spilling the beans," Dad tells me as I hand him the roll of tape. "Mom's really going to be surprised."

"Of COURSE I didn't tell her—you told me not to."

Dad laughs. "That hasn't stopped you before." He doesn't have to bring up Christmas two years ago, when he bought Mom a pendant she used to admire in the window of a jewelry store downtown. He didn't have it in the house one day before I blurted out his secret, ruining the

pendant

Christmas-morning moment he'd planned. Mom was happy to get the necklace a month early but Dad was annoyed.

While everyone quietly waits for Mom to show up, Matt pulls me aside and asks if I've talked to Carly. "She can't find anyone to play John Adams."

"The guy did a million things—like sign the Declaration of Independence," I say. "But Carly wants him to sit at a desk reading letters! It's stupid!" I lower my voice. "I haven't talked to her—is she okay?"

"Besides scrambling to find a new actor, I guess so."

This doesn't answer my question and I can feel myself turning red. "If you feel so bad, why don't YOU play John Adams? And why are you so worried about Carly all of a sudden?"

Matt shrugs. "I was the one who volunteered you and now she's stuck, that's all."

I don't tell Matt but I've been thinking the same thing. It's been weird not talking to Carly these past couple of days but that still doesn't mean I want to read stupid love letters onstage. I wish we could fast-forward past this and be friends again.

Nancy and Charlie shush the crowd when Mom's car pulls into the driveway. Everybody hides behind filing cabinets and desks until Mom enters the office and we all yell, "Surprise!" For a moment, my always-has-something-to-say mom is speechless; she clasps her

clasps

hands in front of her face and tears form in the corners of her eyes. She finally finds words and thanks everyone for remembering her birthday.

Her employees all brought joke presents—a poodle coffee mug and a singing goldfish pen—but Dad and I save our presents for later. He got her a set of books on the history of jazz and I got her a gift card so she could download music to go along with the book. Matt drew a hasty card, raided his own mom's linen closet, and found an expensive bar of soap wrapped in floral paper with a bow. Mom puts her arm around Dad and seems moved by the whole event.

Charlie's sitting on one of the chairs by the door, sketching. I plop

download

hasty

down beside him to take a look at his work.

He points to different people in the room and the caricature he drew of each of them. The one of Nancy is the funniest, with her large glasses and space between her front teeth. Charlie's drawings are so good, I'm embarrassed to show him my own. When he asks to see them, I tell him my notebook's in the house, even though it's inside my bag just a few feet away.

caricature

Nancy calls Charlie over so they can take a group photo. Mom beams, while Dad crams the staff into the picture. As everyone jokes around, I flip through more of Charlie's caricatures; the one he did of Dad captures his smile perfectly. When I get to the illustration in the back of

crams

the book, I'm more surprised than my mother was an hour ago when she walked into the party.

The page is covered with a familiar Minotaur grinning up at me.

What to Do

I've learned enough in my brief time with Sensei Takai to know that jumping to conclusions is very un-ninja. There could be plenty of reasons Charlie has drawings of a Minotaur in his notebook but it's coincidental that out of the billion things to draw, he chose the exact subject the vandal did. The sensible thing to do is to share my suspicions

sensible

with Dad, but since when do I do the sensible thing?

Instead I let Matt in on my theory.

"A few days ago, you thought it was Umberto!" Matt says. "Charlie doesn't seem like the kind of guy to sneak out in the middle of the night to vandalize buildings. He seems more of the stay-home-watch-TV-and-wish-I-had-a-girlfriend kind of guy."

I agree but tell him that doesn't explain the drawing in Charlie's sketchpad. I suggest we follow him after the party.

"Hopefully we can get to the bottom of things without running into Mr. Demetri."

I shudder just thinking about getting caught by our principal again.

My parents sit in the waiting room chairs talking to the party-goers who are still here. I COULD drag Dad away and tell him about Charlie's drawing but asking to talk to him privately in front of five other people would definitely be awkward.

When I see Charlie tying a clip on the bottom of his pants, I hurry to find Matt.

"Charlie biked here! We CAN follow him!"

We say a quick good-bye to my parents and I tell them I'll be back soon. Matt and I pretend to fix our bikes in the driveway but what we're really doing is waiting for Charlie to jump on his. As soon as he does, Matt and I pedal behind him at a safe distance.

"Suppose he lives twenty miles away?" Matt whispers. "My mother will freak if I'm not home by dark."

We make a deal that we won't follow Charlie if he goes too far from either of our homes. As soon as we make the pact, Charlie pulls over and ties his bike to a rack in front of a coffee shop next to the high school. The sign on the red awning reads FROM THE GROUND UP.

awning

Matt and I throw our bikes on the grass and watch Charlie from across the street.

"We're totally being ninjas," Matt says. "Finally."

I gesture to the building behind us. "The high school was the second place in town that got vandalized. And it's right across from where Charlie goes for coffee."

"We don't know if he comes here all the time," Matt says.

"Yes, we do." Through the window, we watch a waiter bring over a cup to Charlie's table. "He didn't have to order," I say. "He's a regular."

Matt smiles, impressed by my ninja detective skills.

"How long do we sit here and watch one of your mom's employees drink coffee?" Matt asks.

I shrug. "Until we find out if he's the vandal."

"More like until we get bored."

Matt and I take turns on the stakeout—one of us watches Charlie while the other plays games on my phone. As I watch Charlie sketching in his notebook through the coffee shop window, I think about Carly. She's put in so much work, it

stakeout

seems a shame for the whole pro-duction to go down the toilet because of me.

I nudge Matt when Charlie packs up his things. I expect him to hop on his bike but he doesn't. He walks out of the coffee shop, stretches, and heads across the street—directly toward us.

Without a word, Matt and I duck behind a row of hedges.

"Do you think he saw us?" Matt whispers.

I shake my head, still watching Charlie approach. He passes by our hiding place and walks around the perimeter of the school.

"He's going back to the scene of the crime!" I whisper.

Sure enough, when we sneak around the corner, Charlie's standing

in front of the Minotaur mural, taking in the whole scene.

"Admiring his handiwork," I say.

handiwork

"You and I stood here looking at
the mural too and WE didn't do it,"
Matt says.

"That's 'cuz we were trying to
figure out who did," I answer. "What's
Charlie's excuse?"

"There's no evidence—you're letting your imagination run wild like
you did with Umberto," Matt says.

That's another thing about best
friends—they know just what to say
to shut you up.

Espionage in the Woods

telepathic

It's only been three days since Carly and I had our fight but it feels like forever. With her telepathic parent powers, Mom knows something's up. After avoiding her questions, I finally tell her what happened.

"A nice apology goes a long way," Mom says.

For some reason this feels like girlfriend advice and I feel myself blush.

"The longer you go without fixing this," Mom continues, "the harder it will be."

I'm sure Mom knows what she's talking about but it still seems weird taking her advice. Are Carly and I just supposed to pretend nothing happened?

As if she's reading my mind—again!—Mom smiles across the kitchen table. "Carly's a very special friend—you really don't want to lose her."

My face burns; I've got to get out of here. I pretend I have to go to the bathroom and race out of the room.

"Text her before she texts you!" Mom calls after me.

As uncomfortable as the discussion was, I AM worried about losing Carly as a friend. After lots

physical

tackle

improve

of back and forth, I decide to take Mom's advice and text her a quick "Hi." She immediately texts back and asks how Frank and Bodi are doing in this heat. The sense of relief I feel is almost physical; who knew moms could be so right about things?

Now that the Carly situation is settled, the next subject to tackle is the Minotaur. After talking with Matt yesterday, I've given up on Umberto as the vandal—not one of my brightest ideas. I have absolutely no evidence on Charlie either, just a hunch. But if I DO tell my parents, Mom might be able to watch Charlie at work. I decide to stay quiet and keep my eyes and ears open when Charlie comes to work on Monday. In the meantime, I vow to improve my ninja ways. I sleep in my tie-dyed shinobi shozoku, even wearing my tabi boots in case I have to pounce on an enemy in the middle of the night. Instead of checking the time on my phone, I squint into the sun and try to guess what time it is. (Yesterday I was off by several hours; I definitely need more practice.)

But there's one ninja skill I discovered I'm surprisingly GOOD at: my sense of direction. I beg Dad to take me to the woods to practice. On Sunday, he takes Matt, Carly, and me to some hiking trails in the Hollywood Hills. He'll work in a nearby coffee shop with Felix while the three of us practice our survival skills. Technically we're only half a mile from Dad, but we PRETEND we just have our wits to rely on.

It's been a while since I ran

survival

through the woods with friends—usually my parents are the ones who drag me to the mountains for hikes. Today, Carly, Matt, and I climb trees, cross streams, and even blindfold ourselves to see if we can find our way back to home base. Several hikers look at us strangely as Carly and I spin Matt around, then take off into the woods. Matt counts to thirty and removes his blindfold. Both Carly and Matt eventually find their way back, but I bound up the hill in seconds flat like a guided missile that knows exactly where to go.

guided

missile

forage

Of course REAL ninjas would forage for berries, nuts, and roots but we brought snacks from home. Instead of sitting on the ground, we climb an oak tree and hang out there.

Carly leans back against the branch, eating her granola bar. "I don't know why we don't come here more often—it's so beautiful."

Neither Matt nor I say anything but I can tell he's thinking the same thing I am. Carly is fearless. She was the first one up the tree and grabbed the highest branch. It's such a weird combination to be a teacher's-pet kind of kid while also being unafraid of pretty much anything. As I watch her tuck the granola wrapper neatly into her pocket instead of tossing it to the ground, I wish I knew more people like Carly; we may have our differences but she's great and I'm glad things with us are back to normal.

unafraid

Matt, of course, has to pretend he's Frank and act like a monkey while he's up here, tossing acorns on a few runners down below. (For the record, Frank doesn't do that.)

After we climb down, we practice the moves we learned at the dojo to prepare for the upcoming competition we found out about yesterday. Matt brings up my toilet-paper fiasco with Sensei Takai and I'm embarrassed when he makes me give a

detailed

detailed account. It's not the kind of story Carly usually thinks is funny, so I'm surprised when she laughs hysterically, which makes me stretch it out for bigger laughs. I grab handfuls of leaves and dive onto the ground re-enacting the escapade. For kids who are here to practice being ninjas, we sure are acting like goofballs.

We head down the trail to meet up with Dad and his colleague. Felix shows us some sketches he's done for the advertising campaign he and Dad are working on—a new energy drink. The characters are bold and angular and I wonder if I'll ever be as good an artist as either him or Dad.

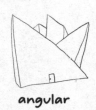

angular

On the drive back, Carly talks about Ms. McCoddle getting married and her mom's new truck but doesn't mention she's having a hard time finding a replacement for John Adams. Either Matt's been exaggerating or Carly's moved on. The traffic's unusually light, so we get home quickly; by the time Carly's ready to jump out of the car, I make a quick decision.

replacement

"If you haven't found anyone yet, *I'll* be John Adams. I don't want to leave you in the lurch."

Matt raises his eyebrows and, for

once, waits to see what happens before jumping in.

Carly shrugs and says okay, as if it doesn't matter at all.

"I mean, I don't HAVE to," I say.

"Whatever you want," she responds. "It's up to you."

shift

Matt's eyes shift from me to Carly like he's watching a tennis match.

This time I'm the one who shrugs. "Whatever."

Carly thanks my dad for the ride and runs up the walkway to her house.

"What just happened?" Matt asks. "Are you doing or NOT doing the play?"

I have no idea.

A Rash Decision

The next morning, I can tell something's amiss before I open my eyes. My entire body feels as if it's on fire.

amiss

I pull up the legs of my pajamas to find my calves covered in a bright red rash. My arms too.

"MOM!"

She comes in with her coffee, ready to hustle me off to school—until she sees me. She puts on the reading glasses that always dangle from the neckline of her shirt and examines my legs.

"Looks like somebody picked up poison oak in the woods."

My mind flashes back to yesterday when I rolled around in the leaves. This is what I get for hamming it up in front of my friends.

Mom grabs my hand before it's moved an inch. "No scratching!" She heads to the bathroom to get some supplies but whips around to catch me ready to scratch again. "I'm not kidding, Derek. Scratching only makes it worse and it could get infected."

It's like my hands have a mind of their own—all they want to do is scratch. Mom orders me into a hot bath, then later covers me with lotion and bandages. I feel like a two-year-old.

"How long will this last?" I ask.

"Usually five to ten days."

"What?! There's a competition at the dojo on Saturday! And I might be in a play!"

Mom's not too sure what to make out of that one. "Then I suggest you get back in bed and don't scratch." She tucks her glasses into the top of her shirt and smiles. "How about if I make you some pumpkin pancakes before I head next door? I think the intelligent thing to do is stay home today."

intelligent

The good news is I don't have to go to school. The bad news is there's no way I'll do well in the competition. As it is now, it hurts just to lie here, never mind kicking and punching.

restraint

"You keep saying being a ninja is more than fast moves," Mom says. "Today you can practice *inner* ninja skills like discipline and restraint."

"Sounds fun."

She laughs and tells me she'll be back up with breakfast in a few minutes. Dad must've left for work early because he would've been in here by now if he were home.

I text Matt and Carly to see if either of them stepped through the poison oak but they're both fine and on their way to school. I can tell Carly feels bad; with a landscaper for a mom, she knows how painful poison oak can be.

repulsive

Matt, of course, thinks it's hilarious and begs me to text him pictures as the rash gets more repulsive.

"Once it blisters, you can pop them," he says. "It'll be more fun than Bubble Wrap."

I know Mom would kill me if I did. When you grow up with a doctor for a mom, there are certain things you know you can and cannot do.

"Here you go." Mom places the tray she only uses when one of us is sick at the foot of the bed.

Luckily the rash hasn't affected my appetite; I devour all four pancakes in a matter of minutes.

devour

I spend most of the day with Frank and Bodi watching martial arts videos online. Frank seems to like them as much as the Westerns we watch on TV. Bodi's content just lying on the rug under the table while I try to use the remote without scratching.

Even with videos and food and

music, it feels like an evil witch doctor placed me under an itching curse. Mom makes me cut my fingernails before she goes to the office to make sure I won't rip open any blisters. She even goes a step further and bandages my hands, so it looks like I'm wearing mittens, even though the temperature outside is a balmy seventy-eight degrees.

balmy

The entire day comes down to scratching or not scratching. All I want to do is rip off these bandages and scream.

After watching tons of videos, I decide to use some of my time wisely—not doing homework (duh!)— by checking out photos of the Minotaur murals online. There are several, but the one from a local parents' group is a good one and

I study it closely. I then research different sites of local graffiti artists to see if I can spot someone with a similar style.

A few of the artists also use mythological characters but not in the same style as the school vandal. One artist in particular uses the same colors and tones as the Minotaur guy but his characters are completely different. I return to the photos of the Minotaurs and zoom in to see if the artist left a signature. (They're called tags in the graffiti world—I told you I did some research.)

I enlarge one of the images and print it on Dad's high-end printer so I can see it more clearly. The individual letters are barely legible; all I can make out is that one of them looks like a Minecraft crossbow. Is

legible

crossbow

squishing

Chihuahua

shriveled

it a *W*? An *M*? I squint to read the letters but can't. If the mystery artist is trying to hide his identity by squishing the letters of his signature, his plan is working.

At lunchtime, Mom brings me a grilled cheese sandwich with a bowl of tomato soup (good), then insists I take another hot bath (bad). While I'm in the tub, she gets an emergency call from the office; a Chihuahua a few blocks away just got hit by a car. She tells me to enjoy the bath and she'll be back to reapply bandages as soon as she can. After fifteen minutes, I'm bored and shriveled like a raisin and have to dry off carefully. When I catch my reflection in the mirror, my skin is raw like a zombie, so I have no choice but to act like one.

As I wait for Mom, I get an idea. I grab the poison oak lotion from the counter and slather it on my rash. But the great part of the idea is the second part—instead of bandages, I'll wrap myself head to toe in my ninja gear. Centuries of ninjas can't be wrong—the uniform helps keep you focused and lets you know who you are, like a fireman or a Marine. With my face mask, hood, tabis, and shinobi shozoku, I grab some bologna for Frank and Bodi and settle in to watch more videos.

"WHAT ARE YOU DOING?" Mom screams.

"Practicing my mental discipline, like you said."

She's in her scrubs and hopping mad. "You dyed those ninja clothes, right? Dye comes off with heat and you've got open wounds! You could get an infection! Why couldn't you just wait in your robe till I got back?"

She helps me take off my shinobi shozoku, examines my skin—it's beyond embarrassing—then makes me take the third bath of the day.

The ninja competition is in five days and I'm swaddled in front of the TV like a baby. Matt's going to kick my butt.

swaddled

Itchy Ninja

I end up missing two days of school. Dad works from home to hang out with me but has to take a million phone calls from Felix instead. By the end of the week, I'M the one who needs an energy drink. Dad says Mom's the expert and I have to get her blessing to be able to go to the competition on Saturday. After examining me for the billionth time, she tells me I can go.

blessing

Matt and I are the first ones at the dojo Saturday morning. He's only here because today's the competition and he knows he'll whoop me. I don't bother arguing because OF COURSE HE WILL.

We warm up with kicks and punches but it hurts for me to move. Mom made me promise I'd "take it easy," and for once, I listen. (It's not like I have a choice; I can barely raise my legs.) Matt goes back and forth between concerned friend and throwing it in my face that he's going to kill me.

concerned

Everyone silently lines up when Sensei Takai enters the dojo. I'm still embarrassed from the grocery store incident and don't make eye contact. He doesn't either.

The first part of the competition

is sparring, so we each put on our pads, headgear, and mouthpiece.

mouthpiece

It takes me longer to put on my stuff than it does to compete; Karen knocks me out in less than a minute. Whose bright idea was it for me to come today? Oh, yeah. Mine.

I spend most of the competition sitting on the sidelines watching everyone else have fun. Sensei Takai takes notice of me from the front of the room.

"The last part of the competition will test inner strength," he announces. "All students will stand quietly until the bell."

Everyone looks around, confused. Isn't the whole point of a competition to practice our moves? Matt's the most bewildered of all and raises his hand. Sensei Takai ignores his question and nods for us to begin.

As usual, everyone fidgets—we all want to be moving—but this is one section of the competition I CAN do. After such strenuous activity, standing in one place is actually a relief.

strenuous

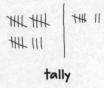

tally

An eternity later, Sensei Takai nods for us to stop, then directs his assistant to tally the scores.

Matt's been practicing, so it makes sense he wins the sparring section of the tournament. Karen's aim has been great from day one, so no one's surprised she aced the section on kicking. But when Sensei Takai softly calls my name as the winner of the discipline segment, everyone is shocked.

He calls the three of us to the

front of the room and ceremoniously places ribbons around our necks. I feel like an Olympian, which is funny considering I just stood still to win.

pursue

"Pursue the silence," Sensei tells me as I join the rest of the class.

It's probably good advice, but all I can think about is how much this ribbon itches.

Dress Rehearsal

On Monday, there are history and science quizzes but I'm focused on spying on Charlie as soon as I get home.

Carly's got something else in mind. "Ready for dress rehearsal?"

"You never told me I was officially back in!"

She smiles. "I just assumed you were."

"Then why didn't you TELL me?"

She shakes her head. "Why is there always so much drama with you?"

I'm ready to scream at the top of my lungs until Carly bursts out laughing. I wait for her laughter to subside.

subside

"Calm down," she finally says. "Rehearsal's at three."

I will never understand girls. Never.

When I text Mom after school, I casually ask what time the office closes today and if Charlie's working. I'm relieved when she texts back "5—yes." There hasn't been a new mural in weeks and I wonder if the vandal's attention has waned. But if it IS Charlie, I'll be there to catch him in the act.

waned

Because I haven't been to a lot of rehearsals, I'm kind of behind, which doesn't make me feel too bad since it's a state of mind I'm familiar with. I check out the other kids and try to follow along.

patriot

The play opens with Farida playing a patriot named Hannah Arnett, whom I've never heard of before.

narrator

Umberto is the narrator, so he's on the side of the stage. "In the Revolutionary War, lots of women helped behind the lines. One of them was an unsung hero named Hannah Arnett."

The curtain opens to reveal the inside of a small cabin. I'm shocked with what Carly and the others have been able to pull off in less than a month. I recognize the old oak table from the art room; the other pieces are probably donations.

Farida addresses the pretend audience.

"I'm Hannah Arnett. My husband, Isaac, and I live in New Jersey. The war hasn't been going well and he and his friends are deciding whether to throw in the towel and join the British. They're actually thinking about giving up!"

Several kids yell, "Boo!" at the thought of surrender. I might actually have been missing out on some fun by not coming to rehearsals.

Farida points to the boys on the stage. "My husband and his friends are thinking about signing a proclamation pledging their loyalty to Britain in exchange for not losing their property."

Farida gets the rest of us to "Boo!" even louder this time.

proclamation

She crosses her arms and lets the suspense build. "But luckily for the patriots, I'm really good at *nagging*."

The rest of the cast laughs before Farida bursts into song.

I grab Carly in a panic. "IS THIS A MUSICAL NOW?"

She ignores me and focuses on Farida, who's doing a great job singing a song called "War Is Nothing Compared to How Much I'm Going to Bug You." During her solo, the boys onstage are hilarious—hiding under the table, covering their ears, pretending not to listen. It's a big comedy number that Farida nails.

Am I going to have to sing too?

I try to make eye contact with Carly but she doesn't notice.

THIS IS A DISASTER!

Umberto takes the stage. "You've all heard of me," he begins. "I'm Paul Revere—the silversmith from Boston who made a famous midnight ride to warn the colonists the British were coming."

Umberto looks great in his tricornered hat and jacket with silver buttons. His wheelchair has an awesome papier-mâché horse head attached to the front.

tricornered

"Here's a fun fact," Umberto continues. "I never yelled, 'The British are coming! The British are coming!' Who wants to hear what I *really* yelled when I took that famous ride?"

"I never would've yelled 'The British are coming' because we colonists thought of *ourselves* as British. What I *really* yelled was, 'The

Regulars are coming out!' Because *Regulars* meant 'the army'!" Umberto zips across the stage in his wheelchair as if he's on a horse like Paul Revere.

The rest of the cast members clap and cheer him on. "RIDE. RIDE. RIDE. RIDE!"

Suddenly Darcy slides down the ramp in her own wheelchair with horse head. I burst out laughing. What a creative way to get horses onstage.

"I'm Sybil Ludington," Darcy says. "I'm only sixteen but I rode forty miles through the night—alone!—to warn colonists in Connecticut."

Carly has to tell Darcy and Umberto to focus on the scene; they're so busy zipping around in their dueling wheelchairs they miss their musical cue.

dueling

I've talked to or texted Umberto every day for a week and not once did he mention the play called for singing! The power of his voice takes me by surprise. It's low and strong; when he and Darcy harmonize on the chorus, a chill runs up my arm. Umberto is the REAL ninja—totally full of surprises.

harmonize

Carly tells everyone to take a ten-minute break and I hurry over.

"Since when is this a musical?!" I whisper-shout. "The only thing possibly worse than reading love letters is SINGING love letters! You didn't tell me on purpose!"

A slow smile creeps over Carly's face. "Matt, Umberto, and I thought it would be a nice surprise."

hatched

scheming

The idea that my friends hatched a plan to get me to sing in front of the whole school leaves me speechless. Since when is Carly one of the guys, coming up with pranks behind my back?

I jump when Carly reaches for my hand. "You don't have to be in the play if you don't want to. You know that, right?"

I'm horrified someone might see Carly's hand touching mine but I'm also reassured that even though she was scheming behind my back, she still has my best interests at heart.

"I'm in," I tell her. "Looks like you and the cast have been enjoying yourselves."

"I guess Matt and Umberto each

owe me a dollar," Carly says. "I *told* them you'd do it."

"Wait, what? I thought I was being unpredictable!"

Carly blows the whistle around her neck to get everyone's attention. That girl is five hundred times smarter than the rest of us, hands down.

Time to Spy

duet

Rehearsal ends up running long, so I thankfully don't have to sing a song I don't even know in front of the entire cast. Before we leave, Carly hands me the lyrics to the song she and I will rehearse tomorrow.

"Does this mean we're doing a duet?" I ask.

"That's usually what it's called when two people sing the same song," she laughs.

I shove the lyrics into my back pocket and hurry home. Hopefully following Charlie tonight will make up for that stupid rehearsal.

When I walk in the kitchen, Dad's cutting up broccoli and cauliflower at the counter. I toss my pack in the corner and grab some veggies for the road.

cauliflower

"You going out?" Dad asks.

I look at the kitchen clock and tell him I'm going to ride my bike around the neighborhood.

"I'll go with you." Dad places the veggies in a bowl and rinses the cutting board.

"You want to ride bikes with me?" IS HE KIDDING?

"Sure—I could use some fresh air."

I can't remember the last time

urge

sheepishly

Dad and I rode bikes together; why does he suddenly have the urge to exercise when I'm on my way to a stakeout?

He looks at me sheepishly. "Your mom thought it was strange that you asked if Charlie was working. She wants to make sure you're not up to something."

"ME?"

Dad dries his hands on the dish towel. "Is this some new ninja mission? And why Charlie?"

It's no use trying to keep this from Dad; he and Mom have always been mind-reading aliens from another planet. Most of the time it's just easier to surrender. I grab another handful of veggies, sit at the table, and tell Dad the whole story.

When I'm finished, he seems confused. "Just because Charlie was staring at the mural and made a few sketches doesn't make him the vandal. But it *is* a fluke—I'll give you that."

fluke

"I thought I'd follow him and see if he goes to another crime scene."

Dad checks a text, then puts his phone in his pocket. "Let me come with you. What did Felix call it—a ninternship? You can be the sensei today."

Performing acts of espionage isn't the same when one of your parents tags along. But Dad insists, so we get our bikes out of the garage and wait in the backyard for Charlie to come out.

At five on the dot, Charlie comes out of the office, slips his bag over his shoulder, and jumps on his bike.

Dad and I follow.

I am the sensei!

You Call This Spying?

As much as it's ludicrous to tail a suspect with your father, I have to admit, it's also kind of fun. Lately, Matt, Umberto, and I have been practicing hand gestures like real ninjas, so I use some of them now. Dad gets a little carried away, making up silly hand motions and almost falling off his bike twice. Even with all the theatrics, we ride through the streets unseen by Charlie.

theatrics

At least I think so.

After about a mile, Charlie pulls his bike alongside a stretch of grass behind one of the parking garages at UCLA. Dad and I look on as Charlie takes out his sketchbook, leans against a tree, and starts drawing.

We're several yards away but excessive talking is prohibited for ninjas, so Dad and I hide behind some cars where we can talk.

Dad holds up his phone and shows me a text. It's Mom wanting to know if we're having fun.

"This isn't supposed to be fun!" I whisper. "We're spies!"

Dad winks and puts his phone away. "Just because Charlie's sketching doesn't mean he's planning the next mural. He could be drawing

prohibited

pictures of cows in a pasture for all we know."

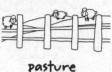
pasture

Technically that's true, but my ninja radar tells me Charlie has something else in mind.

And then it hits me.

I gesture to the giant concrete wall Charlie's facing. "That's where the next mural will be."

Dad looks at the three-story wall of white cement. "It's a great blank canvas, that's for sure." He turns to me. "This is still just a theory—but maybe we should formulate a plan."

formulate

It's nice having a sidekick, even if it is your dad.

Yet Another Surprise

Mom, of course, thinks Dad and I are being RIDICULOUS.

"Charlie's not the one drawing Minotaurs all over town," she says.

"I don't know, honey," Dad says. "Tonight things seemed a little fishy to me too."

Mom takes Frank out of his cage. I don't have to ask why—I can smell his soiled diaper from across the room. Thankfully, she doesn't hand

soiled

him to me but takes him next door to her office instead. When she comes back, she's not only with Frank but Felix.

labyrinth

"Here are the sketches you wanted for the Labyrinth promotion." Felix hands Dad a folder full of papers.

"Worst name for an energy drink ever," Mom says. She offers Felix a cup of tea.

"Hey, Derek, how's your ninternship going?" Felix asks.

I know ninjas never blab but I can't help telling Felix about the spying session I just had with Dad.

Felix laughs. "You guys spied on one of your mom's employees? On your bikes? What did this guy do— assault someone?"

assault

My mother rubs Frank's head

before putting him back in his cage. "I told Derek there's no way Charlie's responsible for those Minotaurs."

Felix almost does a spit-take. "What's a Minotaur?"

I pull up a picture of the mythical beast on my phone and give him the details of the case.

Felix smiles. "Maybe those ninja lessons are paying off."

Dad gives Felix notes on his sketches and makes plans for their meeting next week. I'd love to sit around and talk about ninjas all night but I have rehearsal tomorrow and don't want to look like an idiot.

memorize

I spend the rest of the night trying to memorize the lyrics to the song I'm supposed to sing with Carly. When did she and the other kids have time to write these songs anyway? Fortunately our song is short, unlike Farida's and Umberto's, which are several verses long. I've been worried the song would be sappy and lame but it's actually kind of funny, as if John and Abigail Adams were partners in crime during the Revolution.

After school the next day, Carly and I rehearse before the other kids arrive. I can't remember if she's ever heard me sing before and I start to feel pools of perspiration underneath my T-shirt.

perspiration

"Don't worry," Carly says. "You'll be great."

Carly's enthusiasm, as always, is contagious and I get into the role, gesturing along with the lyrics.

But when we finish, Carly isn't

notch

oxymoron

as thrilled as I thought she'd be. "Uhm...maybe you can take it down a notch," she says. "Your performance was a little big."

"'Little big' is an oxymoron," I say. "A real director would never say that."

"Okay, how's this? You're over-acting."

"ME?" I pace the stage, exaggerating as I walk. "I am John Adams and I write letters to my wife because I'm most happy when she's not in the same room with me."

Carly blushes, so I can tell I hit a nerve. She crosses her arms in front of her and tells me the rest of the cast will be here in a few minutes. "We'll run through the song one more time—you'll be fine for Friday."

"What's Friday?"

She looks ready to explode. "The play!"

"THIS Friday? I thought it was next week!"

Carly shakes her head. "You didn't read any of the emails from Ms. McCoddle about the date change?"

I admit I didn't even open them.

"Well, I guess you'll just have to cram," Carly says.

Story of my life.

Lying in Wait

programming

After I fill in Matt and Umberto with the latest on the Minotaur case, I ask who wants to come with me on tonight's stakeout. But Umberto has a programming class and it's Matt's parents' anniversary party, so neither of them can come.

"How about Friday?" Matt asks. "I'm free then."

"He'll be at the play," Umberto says. "We all will."

Right...

"Come on, guys—I don't want to spy with my dad again!"

It's no use. Looks like tonight's mission is up to the Fallon ninjas.

But when I get home, Dad's still at the office working on his company's new product promotion. It'll be dark soon, so Mom won't let me go out on my own. Unless, of course, I'm going to Matt's parents' anniversary party....

promotion

Lying to my mother isn't something I make a habit of—mostly because 99 percent of the time she ends up finding out the truth. I could ask her to come with me on the stakeout, but I can't see her agreeing to spy on someone who works for her. After a quick internal

internal

debate, I tell her I'll be at Matt's and run upstairs to change.

"Why are you wearing your shinobi shozoku to an anniversary party?" Mom asks when she sees me.

I knew I should've changed after I left. To get out of this new dilemma, I pile another lie on top of my original one and tell her the anniversary party is a masquerade.

She looks at me suspiciously.

"I think it's a great idea. Matt's mom is going as Wonder Woman and his dad's dressing up as Superman." The lies come pouring out as I make up costumes for Matt's entire family. (I'm not sure his Gram would appreciate the fact that I embellish the story further by having her dress up as Little Bo Peep.)

embellish

Mom grabs her purse. "I'll drive you over so I can congratulate Jill and Tom. Sounds like quite the party."

"No!" I realize my reaction is over the top and dial it down. "I mean, it's just a few blocks away—I can ride my bike."

She thinks about it and puts down her purse. "Text me when you're ready to come home and we'll throw your bike in the trunk."

I tell her okay, hoping I'll be at the police station handing over the vandal by then.

By nature I'm pretty impatient, but part of Sensei Takai's philosophy has definitely rubbed off on me. I'm actually looking forward to being outside and just waiting—a totally new feeling. The fact that I'll be waiting up in a tree like a real ninja

philosophy

makes the whole thing that much more thrilling.

When I was home sick those days, I mapped out the places where the graffiti artist had struck, and this large wall at UCLA is located dead center. I'm not saying the vandal will come tonight—or at all—I'm just saying if I were looking for a blank canvas in the same neighborhood, this is where I'd be.

remnants

I still have remnants from the rash, so before climbing the tree, I make sure there's no poison oak around the base. A few runners and skateboarders pass by but no one pays any attention to the giant wall.

I'd be lying—again—if I said I wasn't bored after thirty minutes. I'd love to play a game on my phone, but even with the sound off, the light coming off the screen would give away my position. I try to sing the lyrics of John and Abigail Adams's song in my head but can't remember more than the first two lines.

There's a noise on the path and for a split second my mind flashes to Umberto. It was wrong to jump to conclusions about him; there are a dozen reasons why he could've had a can of paint that day. I'd apologize to him if the whole idea weren't completely embarrassing.

This time the noise is closer. Judging by the darkness, it's probably nine o'clock, earlier than I thought the artist would show up. But the wall is so vast, I guess he'd have to start early if he wanted to finish tonight. Sure enough, a figure

vast

steps out from the trees. Is it Charlie?

There's not a lot of light so I can't make out much besides the fact that it's a guy with a bag slung over his shoulder. He kneels on the grass and pulls out several spray cans and some folded-up papers, probably stencils. His back is to me so I can't see his face. All I want to know is if it's Charlie.

discovered

As he prepares to work, I decide I should call 911, but I'm so close, there's no way I could call without getting discovered. I have to remind myself to breathe.

The vandal steps into the light and I can't help but gasp.

He's wearing head-to-toe ninja clothes.

Like me!

His aren't tie-dyed, which leaves out Matt. (I have to stop suspecting my friends.)

suspecting

Does Charlie have a shinobi shozoku? I get an even worse thought—could the mystery artist be Sensei Takai? Why would he paint murals all over town? Whoever it is, vandalizing is SO un-ninja.

I take another deep breath as the artist tapes his stencil to the wall. The paper is so large and unwieldy, part of me wants to jump down and help him. But the vandal works quickly and within a few minutes the wall is ready to paint.

unwieldy

I'm surprised when he starts at the bottom right-hand corner of the wall. What kind of artist writes his signature BEFORE he paints? This guy must be incredibly conceited!

conceited

But as soon as he spray-paints the wavy black letters I realize where I've seen this handwriting before. Sure, on the Minotaur photographs I printed out and studied but somewhere else too. Fancy letters—Dad called it calligraphy. Suddenly, I know who the vandal is before he pulls back his hood to wipe the sweat from his forehead.

It's Felix.

Trapped in a Tree

I keep asking myself what a ninja would do in this situation and a realization smacks me in the head. I'm NOT a ninja—I'm a kid in a tree who can't call for help.

realization

As I watch, Felix paints a swath of purple across the white wall. How can I stop him?

swath

In the past month, I've suspected Umberto and Charlie, not to mention lots of other random people, but not once did I suspect Felix. Of course, if I'd been paying attention to details when I looked at his drawings that day, I might not be in this awkward position now.

Much to my disappointment, no one walks by to discover Felix. This really is up to me. I brace myself for the jump down just as Felix finishes the Minotaur's head.

A noise stops me before I jump.

"Put down that paint."

The voice is firm and familiar.

It belongs to my dad.

Felix whips around, still holding the spray can. "Jeremy ... what are you doing here?"

"The question is what are YOU doing here?" Dad points to the cans of paint and stencils on the ground.

I hold my breath, hoping neither of them can hear me.

Dad shakes his head. "I should've recognized the lettering, Felix. But luckily my son realized where you'd strike next."

Of course I thought someone ELSE would show up here, but if Dad's handing out credit, I'm not going to quibble.

quibble

Dad pulls his phone from his pocket.

"There's no need to call the police. I can be gone in a flash." Felix hastily packs up his things.

Dad continues to make the call. "Sorry, Felix. That's not how this plays out. Nice ninja outfit, by the way."

Felix stands tall and faces my dad. "It'll be your word against mine that I was here tonight."

panther

I couldn't ask for a better cue.

Jumping out of the tree like a panther, I land silently beside Felix. Not to brag, but the move is TO-TALLY ninja. "Looks like it's your word against OURS."

In our ninja outfits, Felix and I look like we're on our way to a father-son costume party. But my real dad's the one NOT wearing a costume. He's calling the police instead.

I ask Felix why he's wearing a shinobi shozoku.

brand

He stares down at his tabi boots. "After seeing you and Matt in yours, I thought it would be cool to brand myself as a ninja graffiti artist."

The fact that Felix would actually copy the clothes of a kid like me makes me feel proud and embar-rassed at the same time.

"I don't get it," Dad says. "You have a good job—why are you doing this?"

Felix can't look my father in the eyes. "I AM doing my job. These Minotaurs are promoting the energy drink we've been working on all month."

Dad seems completely lost. "Our campaign's for TV ads, not graffiti. And there's no Minotaur!"

"There is in the social media campaign. These murals have been blowing up on Instagram and Twitter."

Dad shakes his head, still baffled.

baffled

"The company wanted me to do this even before you hired me," Felix says. "Why do you think all the murals are across from schools? Kids are our target market. The agency kept you out of the loop on this part

defeated

of the job—they probably thought you wouldn't approve."

I set my eyes on Felix, who acts like he just defeated my dad in hand-to-hand combat. As much as my father prides himself on being young and cool—for a dad—it's obvious his coworkers don't think of him that way. But it's probably a good thing his agency didn't tell him what they were up to.

Dad's expression turns from confused to knowing. "The product's called Labyrinth—in Greek mythology, that's where the Minotaur was trapped."

My mind flashes back to Ms. Mc-Coddle's class last year. If I'd been paying attention when Dad was talking about his energy drink campaign, maybe I would've made the connection between Labyrinth soda and the Minotaurs.

Felix still isn't giving up. "If you call the police, the advertising company will get in trouble too. You'll probably even get fired, Jeremy."

My father smiles. "So be it."

It doesn't take long before we hear sirens.

Felix won't admit anything to the police; instead, he just keeps asking for his lawyer. Dad and I wait around to give one of the officers a statement. When we're done, Dad throws my bike into the trunk of his car.

statement

"As soon as your mom said you were going to Matt's parents' anniversary party in a ninja outfit, I knew where you'd REALLY be." He smiles. "A stakeout is definitely more fun than an anniversary party, but you shouldn't lie to Mom. You're on your own explaining this to her."

"That's IF I decide to tell her."

"I'm leaving that up to you," Dad says. "I've got some important phone calls to make."

When we get home, I come clean and tell Mom everything—mostly because I'm bursting with the news.

calculated

I calculated where the vandal would be!

I apprehended the bad guy!

I, Derek Fallon, am a super ninja!

apprehended

(With a little help from my dad, of course.)

Carly's Revolution

The next few days are a flurry of information. Dad doesn't get fired from the advertising agency—he quits. No one gets thrown in jail, but Felix and the agency both get fined a LOT of money and have to pay to clean up all the graffiti.

flurry

Umberto and Matt make me tell the story a hundred times about how I used my ninja skills to catch the vandal. (Actually, they don't

MAKE me; I tell the story to anyone who'll listen.) And talking about the Minotaur takes up so much of my time that I don't have a second to spend worrying about the school play.

In all the years I've known her, I've never seen Carly as nervous as she is the night of the play. Umberto tries to help by guiding her through a deep breathing exercise but it's hard not to laugh at a kid teaching meditation when he's dressed like Paul Revere.

meditation

jovial

The auditorium is packed with students, parents, and teachers; it's nice to see Mr. Demetri back to his jovial self since no one's painting Minotaurs on the walls of the school anymore.

Umberto pulls me aside. "I'm not

having any luck with Carly. Do something!"

"Come on, rock star," Matt jokes. "Do your thing."

catatonic

Turns out, what has Carly catatonic isn't standing in front of several hundred people or being the one in charge. It's that she won't do her character justice.

"Who am I to think I can play Abigail Adams?" Carly asks me when no one's around. "She was one of the smartest women of her time. She was married to one president and raised another! She influenced policy!" Carly paces back and forth backstage.

I can't help but smile at seeing Little Miss Perfect so unraveled. "How do you think I feel? I'm playing John Adams!" I lean in next to her

unraveled

until our foreheads touch. "Let's freak out together."

"ARRRGGGHHH!" Carly screams first, then I join in.

Darcy, Farida, and Umberto stare at us in a panic.

When Carly finally stops screaming, she bursts out laughing. "OMG— do you think the audience heard us?"

"I think they heard us in Chicago." I laugh.

Carly squeezes my hand. "Thanks, John Adams."

"No problem, Abigail."

She gathers the cast for a pre-performance cheer then tells Matt to dim the lights and open the curtain.

Our scene isn't till later in the play, so I get to watch the others from backstage for a while. Darcy is going so fast in her wheelchair horse that she almost loses control, which is kind of funny. Umberto's Paul Revere sings about warning the colonists while Darcy's Sybil Ludington bemoans the fact that no one's ever heard of her when Paul Revere's a household name.

bemoans

Farida belts out her Hannah Arnett song with so much force, the audience gives her a standing ovation.

ovation

When it's time for Carly and me to read/sing/perform some of the letters of John and Abigail Adams, a jolt of anxiety shoots up my spine. This time Carly returns the favor and calms me down immediately.

"You ready to have some fun?" she whispers.

nixed

I'm not sure if that'll be possible but I head onstage anyway. I'm so glad I nixed the white wig she wanted me to wear.

With the spotlights on full force, I can't see the faces of the people in the audience, which is a good thing. Carly sits behind the first desk, I take my place behind the second, and Umberto joins us onstage as the narrator.

"Abigail Adams was another woman who played an important role in the American Revolution," Umberto begins. "When the infantry received their first shipment of muskets, they were surprised to find the guns didn't come with bullets or gunpowder. Abigail told her children to gather all the silver and metal in the house. Then she melted them

infantry

muskets

down to make bullets. Her actions impressed the soldiers so much, they snuck into the British camp to steal gunpowder. She really inspired the troops."

There are murmurs from the audience. Most people today probably can't imagine the wife of a statesman being so hands-on.

statesman

Umberto waits for the audience to settle down. "The Second Lady is the woman married to the vice president and Abigail Adams was the *first* Second Lady."

From my seat at the desk I watch Mr. Demetri nod. I'm not sure he knew that fun fact either.

"But Abigail Adams was also the second *First* Lady because her husband John was the second president of the United States." Umberto pops a wheelie, which isn't in the script but gets a laugh from the crowd. "Let me introduce you to Abigail Adams, the first Second Lady and the second First Lady."

He gestures to Carly, who taps the microphone before she speaks. I'm not sure if it's to test the sound or for good luck.

excerpt

"Hello, I'm Abigail Adams. Not only do I help fight for the country's independence, but I'm very out-spoken about women's rights. This is an excerpt from a letter I wrote to my husband on March 31, 1776, as he and other patriots were drafting the Declaration of Independence."

She reads a letter about men not abusing their power, which gets a lot of hoots from women in the audi-ence. I read a letter back about how much Abigail means to me. In the few times we've rehearsed this, the letter felt a little corny but now looking at Carly listening so intently, I can almost identify with John and Abigail Adams. For all our squabbling, Carly and I are friends and partners too.

After we're done reading, we break into the song Carly wrote called "Abigail Adams: Make Those Bullets!" At first, I'm nervous to sing in front of this many people, but when everyone starts clapping along, Carly and I both get into it and have fun. The crowd stands and applauds when we're done. Nice!

THE END
finale

The finale goes off without a hitch and the cast takes several bows.

After the show, Mr. Demetri pulls me aside. I assume it's to tell me my performance was great but instead he thanks me for finding out who was behind the Minotaur graffiti.

"I'm sorry I suspected you and your friends," the principal says. "I should've known you boys weren't behind it."

I want to say *I TOLD YOU!* but just nod.

"Your persistence and follow-through are what helped stop the nonsense," he says. "Nice job, Derek."

And just like that the case of the mysterious Minotaur is officially

terminated

famished

terminated. I guess that's how it goes as you get older. Nice job, then move on to the next thing. Which I'm happy to do because there are food trucks outside and I'm famished.

Master Class

Matt's brother, Jamie, drops us off at the dojo for class. He must be going through some kind of military phase because his head is shaved and he's wearing camouflage shorts. I've known Jamie almost my entire life, but never noticed how much his ears stick out. With the short hair-cut, his ears look like two handles on the sides of a jug. But he's still the

quoting

boisterous

same old Jamie, goofing around and quoting funny lines from movies.

When Sensei Takai quietly takes his place at the front of the room, I'm ready. Today he doesn't make us balance on one foot or stand in silence. He guides us through a series of kicks and punches more difficult than any we've done before. Ten minutes in, most of us are drenched. I can tell everyone's pleased—Matt especially—to be doing these elaborate moves, but I almost miss the quiet of listening. For a kid who's been boisterous his whole life, no one's more surprised by this than I am.

Studying with Sensei Takai has made me focus on other parts of myself too. And the time I've been sitting and listening and practicing silence actually might be helping in the physical world as well, because when I move this time, I kick higher than I've ever kicked before.

"That was awesome," Matt says as we put our shoes on. "I felt like I was in a Hong Kong action movie."

When I look up, Sensei Takai is still at the front of the room. He looks at me with an expression that says he's waiting. I take off my sneakers again and walk toward our teacher.

"Good work today," Sensei Takai says. "Keep practicing. Stay focused."

I nod and wait for more pearls of wisdom but Sensei just bows.

Wait! I thought when he called me over, he might've heard about my part in nabbing the Minotaur guy

nabbing

and he was going to congratulate me. Or how cool it was that I was a real ninja spying from a tree. Or how my ninja practice has helped me grow up a tiny bit. Maybe even that I have all the makings of a sensei too.

But my teacher says none of that. And waiting and hoping for his approval is VERY un-ninja.

I smile at how much work I have left to do in the ninja department.

Sensei Takai smiles as if he knows what I'm thinking.

And he probably does.

All's Well That Ends Well

One of the presents Mom got at her surprise party was a board game about different dog breeds. Turns out the gift was from Charlie and it's pretty fun—even though my sheepdog comes in last every time.

sheepdog

Mom suggests a Sunday-night game night, complete with a giant chicken quesadilla and tortilla soup. Root beer floats don't really fit the

quesadilla

menu, but when I request them, Mom laughs and says okay.

Frank had a cyst behind his right ear earlier in the week, so now his head is bandaged where Mom had to drain it. The procedure certainly didn't drain Frank's energy, though; he bounces on my lap as if he wants to play the board game too. The bandage makes him look like a furry mummy, so I take several photos and send them to Matt. Bodi's exhausted from chasing squirrels before dinner and sleeps on the woven rug my parents brought back from Mexico. It's a quiet, lazy night, which is fine after such a busy week.

When my phone dings with a new text, I assume it's Matt commenting on the picture but it's an unidentified number. Dad motions to the board

woven

unidentified

and tells me it's my turn but I can't stop staring at the new text.

Come outside.

Matt must've grabbed Jamie's phone by mistake when he skateboarded over here. But when I open the back door, it's not Matt on the steps. It's Carly—in full ninja gear.

Her clothes are jet-black—not tie-dyed like mine—and the only things you can see behind her facemask hood are her twinkling brown eyes.

disposable

"I'm going total ninja spy. I even used my dad's disposable phone." She bows deeply; I laugh and bow back.

"Now that the play's over, I thought we could practice some moves in the yard," she says.

"Oh, you mean you don't want

to sit around and read really old letters?"

"The only letters you'll be reading are the get-well cards you'll get in the hospital after I kick your butt." I can't see her mouth, but I know Carly's smiling.

Dad waves me off with a grin and I race upstairs to put on my gear.

Cowabunga!

GOFISH

JANET TASHJIAN

What is your favorite ninja book or movie?
Both Jake and I are old-school martial arts–movie aficionados. We are giant Bruce Lee, Jackie Chan, and Jet Li fans. The fight scene in the room of mirrors in *Enter the Dragon* is one of my favorite action sequences of all time.

Have you ever taken martial arts classes?
I'm more of a yoga person myself, but Jake took Kenpō classes when he was little and got up to a brown belt. When we traveled through China, I loved going to the public parks in the morning and doing Tai Chi with the locals.

What are your favorite parts of *My Life as a Ninja*?
The original title of the book was going to be *My Life as a Secret Agent* or *My Life as a Spy* but my nephew John said, "You should call it NINJA—they were total spies." Because John is one of my favorite people, I started doing research into ninja culture and sure enough, ninjas were great spies. I also love mysteries—*My Life as a Book* has a mystery running through it—so it was fun to watch Derek try and figure out who the vandal was. I'm a big fan of street art and love exploring cities where it's legal. Los Angeles has a big street art scene; I do

graffiti safaris with my friends, so that piece of the book is very much a part of my life.

I also loved writing about Sybil Ludington and the women of the American Revolution. I have such a soft spot in my heart for Carly; she's one of my favorite characters in the series.

How would you finish the line "My life as _____"?
A rewriter. Like most writers, I spend more time rewriting than writing!

Are you more of a reluctant reader like Derek, or are you a big reader?
I'm a massive reader. I've been reading at least three books a week for most of my life. I can't imagine a life without books.

If you could be any living person, who would you be and why?
I'd love to be my son, Jake, for a day to see the world through his eyes. He's got such a great, original view of the world—I'm sure it would be fascinating.

You've traveled around the world. Where would you say your favorite place is?
Where I live. I love Los Angeles. I love the comedy, the music, the restaurants, the beaches, the museums, the mountains, the people. And the weather. I REALLY love the weather.

How did you come up with the My Life series?
Jake used to love books when he was young, but as books became more challenging, reading became difficult. Because he is a visual leaner, he started drawing his vocabulary words on index cards with markers to help in his learning process. When friends would see them, they'd always laugh at how funny

and creative the drawings were. At the same time, I was doing school visits all around the country, listening to teachers, students, and librarians talk about reaching reluctant readers. I wrote *My Life as a Book* for Jake and other kids like him.

If you could be any cartoon character, which one would you be and why?
I mean, who DOESN'T want to be Bugs Bunny? He's unflappable, sarcastic, and has the best comebacks. Bugs totally holds up, even eighty years after he was created.

What's your favorite word Jake has ever illustrated?
It would have to be the word "colleague" from the first book in the series. He drew two guys in prison uniforms on a chain gang, shackled to each other. Brilliant. It still makes me laugh.

Who is your favorite book character and why?
That's an almost impossible question to answer! I love Joey Pigza, I love Arnie the Doughnut, and I love Einstein the Class Hamster. Yes, the last one is one of mine, but he does have a special place in my heart. I'm a sucker for wisecracking characters.

What kind of books do you like to read?
I spend so much time in the fictional world when I'm writing that I end up reading a lot of nonfiction to balance it out. But I also keep up on what my friends are writing, as well as the latest adult fiction. I have a huge collection of vintage children's books, too.

Do you base your characters on people you know?
Sometimes I'll steal a habit or quirk from one of my friends, but never a whole character. It's much more fun to make up characters from scratch.

What is your favorite thing about writing the My Life series?

There are so many things I love about the My Life series, but first and foremost, the greatest part is getting to work with my son. When students ask about our process, I tell them I write the book first, then go through it to highlight age-appropriate vocabulary words, as well as words that would be funny for Jake to illustrate. Then he takes over, drawing more than 220 illustrations for each book in the series. His illustrations literally make me laugh out loud. I love watching him work; he's such a perfectionist and so professional. He's done more than a thousand drawings for this series!

I also like the fact that the books are read by kids all around the world in so many different languages. It's exciting that "reluctant" readers have embraced Derek, his friends, and their crazy adventures. Getting to tell Derek's story is an absolute joy. I find it funny when people talk about what a "bad" kid he is and how he always misbehaves—I know so many boys just like him, and they aren't bad at all!

Are you a fan of cartoons? Do you have a favorite cartoonist? Who and why?

I am a GIANT cartoon nerd. I'm a big fan of watching Saturday morning cartoons—even if it isn't Saturday. We have a cartoon collection that goes all the way back to the 1930s. I love print cartoons, too. Jake and I read *Calvin and Hobbes* in chronological order; it's my favorite comic strip of all time and the reason I dedicated *My Life as a Book* to Bill Watterson. I read every cartoon in *The New Yorker*; Jake reads every *Garfield.* He has a daily cartoon app on his phone so he can keep up with his favorites. I can't imagine a world without cartoons, so it's great to have a cartoonist in the family.

What did you want to be when you grew up?

Students ask me this all the time, and I wish I had a better answer. When I was young, I was too busy playing, reading, and studying to think about career goals. I envy people who knew what they wanted to be by age ten. I was not one of them.

When did you realize you wanted to be a writer?

Before Jake was born I traveled around the world, and when I got back to the States, I had to fill in some forms. One asked for my occupation and I put down "writer," even though I'd never done anything more than dabble. But deep down, I always felt being a writer would be the greatest job in the world. It took me several years after that to make that dream a reality.

What's your first childhood memory?

I remember cooking candies in a little pan on a toy stove that I got for Christmas. I was maybe three. I'm not sure if I remember it or if I just saw the photograph so often that I think I do.

What's your most embarrassing childhood memory?

I was singing and dancing in a school assembly with my first grade class when my shoe fell off. I kept going without the shoe, hopping around the stage—the show must go on.

What was your worst subject in school?

I always did well in school, but for some reason I forgot all my math skills and now can barely multiply. I'd love to know where all my math skills went.

What was your first job?

I've had dozens of jobs since I was sixteen—working on assembly lines, babysitting, washing dishes, waiting tables, delivering dental molds and telephone books, selling copy machines, working in a fabric store, painting houses. . . . I could fill a whole page with how many jobs I've had.

How did you celebrate publishing your first book?
By inviting my tenth-grade English teacher to my first book signing. The photo of the two of us from that day sits on my writing desk.

Where do you write your books?
Usually in my office on my treadmill desk. But because I often write in longhand, I end up writing everywhere—on the beach, in a coffee shop, wherever I am.

When you finish a book, who reads it first?
Always my editor, Christy Ottaviano. We've been doing books together for almost two decades; I consider her one of my closest friends.

How do you usually feel once you've completed a manuscript? Are you ever sad when a book you are writing is over?
Relieved! I don't really miss my characters; they're always with me.

Are you a morning person or a night owl?
I like waking up early and getting right to work. I'm too fried by the end of the day to get anything substantial done.

What's your idea of the best meal ever?
Something healthy and fresh, with lots of friends sitting around and talking. Definitely a chocolate dessert.

Which do you like better, cats or dogs?
I love dogs and have always had one. I'm allergic to cats, so I stay away from them. They don't seem as fun as dogs, anyway.

What do you value most in your friends?
Dependability and a sense of humor. All my friends are pretty funny.

Where do you go for peace and quiet?
I head to the woods. I'm there all the time. I love the beach, too.

What makes you laugh out loud?
My son. He's by far the funniest person I know.

What are you most afraid of?
I worry about all the normal mom things, like war, drunk drivers, and strange illnesses with no cures. I'm also afraid our culture is so invested in technology that we're veering away from basic things like nature. I worry about the implications down the road.

What time of the year do you like the best?
The summer, absolutely. I hate the cold.

If you were stranded on a desert island, who would you want for company?
My family.

If you could travel in time, where would you go?
To the future, to see how badly we've messed things up.

What's the best advice you have ever received about writing?
To do it as a daily practice, like running or meditation.

How do you react when you receive criticism?
My sales background and MFA workshops have left me with a very tough skin. If the feedback makes the book better, bring it on.

What do you want readers to remember about your books?
I want them to remember the characters as if they were old friends.

What would you do if you ever stopped writing?
Try to live my life without finding stories everywhere. For a job, I'd do some kind of design—anything from renovating houses to creating fabric.

What do you like best about yourself?
I'm not afraid to work.

What is your worst habit?
I hate to exercise.

What do you consider to be your greatest accomplishment?
How great my son is.

What do you wish you could do better?
Write a perfect first draft.

What is your idea of fun?
Seeing comedy or music in a tiny club.

Is there anything you'd like to confess?
I love dark chocolate.

What would your friends say if we asked them about you?
She acts like a fifteen-year-old boy.

What's on your list of things to do right now?
EXERCISE!

What do you think about when you're bored?
Story ideas.

How do you spend a rainy day?
Watching comedy.

Can you share a little-known fact about yourself?
I love to make collages.

SQUARE FISH

Can he create his own YouTube web series
and find a way to keep foster monkey
Frank with his family a while longer?

Keep reading for an excerpt.

BEST CLASS EVER

History. Language arts. Geography. Science.

To succeed in any of them, you have to be a pretty good reader—which unfortunately I'm not.

But our school is offering a new after-school elective this winter that doesn't require ANY reading. Plus, the subject is one of my absolute favorite things in the world.

elective

lottery

contain

YouTube!

Because every kid in school wanted to sign up, Mr. Demetri decided to have a lottery. I've never won a raffle in my life, so I was shocked when Ms. McCoddle posted the lucky few students who made the cut and Matt and I were on the list!

Umberto and Carly were on the waiting list—as if anyone's going to drop out of such an awesome elective. And when we find out the teacher is Tom Ennis—a local stand-up comic with his own popular YouTube channel—Matt and I can't contain our excitement. We race down the hallway screaming until Mr. Demetri tells us to knock it off.

"Tom Ennis is HILARIOUS," I tell Matt on our way to the cafeteria. "We're going to have a blast."

Our new teacher's YouTube channel is called LOL Illusions. He's gotten hundreds of thousands of subscribers by being a digital magician like Zach King. Every week he uploads a new video featuring an unbelievable trick. He's not a magician in the traditional sense; instead he's a wizard in post-production who edits his clips with special effects to make them look like magic.

In the 240 videos he's uploaded, he's turned a photo of a kitten into a real kitten in the palm of his hand, he's leaped into a speeding convertible without ever opening the door, he's jumped on his bed so hard he falls through and lands underneath it, and he's thrown a guitar into the dryer and shrank it into an ukulele.

ukulele

Tom's buddy Chris is usually in

the background too, texting on his phone and ignoring Tom as he pulls off these outrageous stunts. The joke is Chris never looks up quick enough to take a picture of the stunt and misses the magic trick every time. It's one of my favorite channels, one that I subscribed to immediately after watching Tom's first clip, where he "makes" dinner by reaching into a cookbook and pulling out a whole turkey.

"Stop rubbing it in," Umberto finally tells us. "I'd give anything to be in that class."

If I added up all the hours Matt, Carly, Umberto, and I have spent watching YouTube, the number would be bigger than all the hours we've logged at school since kindergarten, combined. (The total would be even larger if they'd let us use our phones during class.) But looking at YouTube from the point of view of a CREATOR versus a VIEWER is gigantic. The class starts tomorrow and I already know I'll be up all night, too excited to sleep.

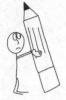

gigantic

When I get home, Mom's in the kitchen putting a casserole in the oven. She must not have a full schedule at her veterinary practice today, because she's in her running clothes instead of her usual scrubs, which means she just got off her treadmill. I try to peek into the oven to see how many vegetables she's hiding in the casserole, but she closes the oven door and asks about my first day back at school after the holiday break.

casserole

I blurt out the news about the

ruckus

prehistoric

YouTube class with so much volume that Dad hurries downstairs.

"What's the ruckus?" he asks. "Are they giving out free puppies at school?"

"Even better." I repeat the story about my new class.

I'm not sure if it's to help celebrate or to show how cool he is, but Dad pulls his phone from his pocket and opens up his YouTube app. "This might be the funniest thing I've ever seen." He holds up the screen and plays a video of David coming back from the dentist. My father's laughing so hard I don't have the heart to tell him how prehistoric that clip is.

It's always hard to concentrate on my homework, but tonight it's especially difficult. Bodi curls underneath the kitchen table as I work, content to just sleep by my feet. Our capuchin, Frank, on the other hand, is jumping around so much, I begin to wonder if he can reach the coffee-pot from his crate.

We've been a foster family for Frank for almost two years, letting him acclimate to humans before going on to monkey college in Boston where he'll learn to help people with disabilities. Every time I think of Frank having to leave, I work myself into such a frenzy that one of my parents has to calm me down. Tonight I'm ALREADY in a frenzy, just thinking about how lucky I am to take part in tomorrow's elective.

YouTube, here I come!

acclimate

OUR VERY OWN
COMEDY NERD

strolls

When Mr. Owens monitored our comedy club elective last year, we looked at him as a necessary evil. With Tom Ennis, however, it's like having a rock star for a teacher. When the final bell rings, every other kid races out of school. But all twelve of us lucky students hurry into another classroom, eager to get started. Tom strolls in ten minutes after school ends, wearing a GoPro camera with an elastic band around his head.

"Hey, kids, I hope you don't mind if I film our sessions."

Not only is he going to teach us— he's going to make us stars! We all sit a little taller in our seats, waiting for our close-ups.

"First of all," he begins, "I'm Tom. But Mr. Demitri INSISTS you guys call me Mr. Ennis, so we'll have to go with that."

He's wearing the skinniest jeans I've ever seen with a beat-up pair of Chuck Taylors. His hair is to his shoulders, with half of it pulled back in a small bun, held up by the band of his camera. His T-shirt is faded and says HAIRY MASTODON, which I'm guessing is a band.

mastodon

Don't miss any of the fun!

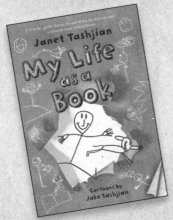

★ "A kinder, gentler Wimpy Kid with all the fun and more plot."
—*Kirkus Reviews*, STARRED REVIEW

★ "Give this to kids who think they don't like reading. It might change their minds."
—*Booklist*, STARRED REVIEW

SQUARE
FISH
MACKIDS.COM